...bang : a novel

002016178

D1481941

DISCARD

bang
BANG

"Brilliant."
Booklist

STARRED ★ REVIEW

When her close friend is shot in the street, the vehemently anti-gun Paula Sherman has no idea what she's in store for. Interviewed by a reporter at the scene, Paula later discovers that her grief-stricken words, taken out of context, are being used by a shady senator and the gun industry to promote the pro-firearm agenda. Suddenly finding herself the unwitting—and very public—proponent of a political stance she abhors, Paula embarks on a decidedly offbeat, one-woman vigilante crusade to bring the gun trade to its knees, a crusade that involves an air pistol and an awful lot of running around (which is OK, because Paula, a waitress whose singing voice has yet to propel her to stardom, could stand to lose a few pounds). Written in the present tense, to give the story additional power, the book is filled with anger and raw urgency. The characters are tough and believable, and the dialogue positively sings. In many ways it's the literary equivalent of a Tarantino movie: edgy, streetwise, and a little arrogant (don't expect a balanced look at the subject of gun control), with a strong and determined female protagonist. Brilliant might be too big a word for this novel but not by much. David Pitt/Booklist

"**bang-BANG** is a stunning accomplishment, a laugh-out-loud, cry-out-loud, terrifying, original and wonderful novel that I simply devoured."
J R Lankford, author, *The Jesus Thief* , (Great Reads Books) an award-winning thriller

"**bang-BANG** is a must-read for people who love guns (they will hate it) and for people who hate guns (they will love the book) . . . **bang-BANG** is a must-read for people who enjoy elegant writing and for those who are into page-turning fiction . . ."
Brigitte Steger, author of the prize winning , *(No) Time to Sleep*

bang
BANG

A Novel by Lynn Hoffman

KÜNATI

b a n g - B A N G

For information, contact Kunati Inc., Book Publishers in both USA and Canada.
In USA: 6901 Bryan Dairy Road, Suite 150, Largo, FL 33777 USA
In Canada: 2600 Skymark Avenue, Building 12, Suite 103, Mississauga, Canada L4W 5B2,
or email to *info@kunati.com*.

F I R S T   E D I T I O N

Designed by Kam Wai Yu
Persona Corp. | www.personaprinciple.com

ISBN 978-1-60164-000-0   LCCN 2006930182
EAN 9781601640000   FIC000000 FICTION/General

Published by Kunati Inc. (USA) and Kunati Inc. (Canada). Provocative. Bold. Controversial.™

h t t p : / / w w w . k u n a t i . c o m

TM—Kunati and Kunati Trailer are trademarks
owned by Kunati Inc. Persona is a trademark owned by Persona Corp.
All other tradmarks are the property of their respective owners.

To

Dr. Judith Sills,

for everything.

Acknowledgements

Thanks to Jamie Lankford, founder of NovelPro
and to Dr. Brigitte Steger. Also to Spencer Hoffman who makes
me hope for a better, saner world.

The video is grainy and the human figures in the centre of a dark stage have grown fuzzy blue-white edges. They seem incandescent, white hot filaments. They are singing, some dozen of them: boys and girls in white shirts and black slacks. Their song claws its way roughly out of the speakers—a windy roar, like a seashell held up to an ear.

Fiddling with the knobs on the monitor, we clean up the sound and lower the contrast. We can now read the banner on the curtain behind the people. It says ALL STATE CHORUS. The stage and its surround may be Carnegie Hall. The song, strained of some of its life, like one of those old-fashioned phonograph recordings, is still astonishingly bright. No raggy imprecision rounds over the edges of their words. Their consonants pop together, all their vowels end with one stoppered breath. The music is Donoff's American Requiem, the old choral standby.

For the solo, Agnus Dei, a girl, eleven or twelve years old, steps forward to a mark on the stage. She looks down, checks her place, her red hair sweeping forward and back as she does. There is humility in the gesture, a tiny bow, a plea for mercy. Then she looks up with wide stallion eyes, quickly sweeps the room, finds the little video camera that made our tape and in looking at it, sings to us.

Her voice has layers to it, youth and age, a discernible, caressable depth. When she sings the words 'I will

take you to my Holy City and I will give you peace,'
we believe her.

Her part ends, the camera jiggles, there is another
roar, applause this time. The girl doesn't acknowledge
it. She steps back in line, head turning quickly to dress
right dress with the other boys and girls.

The song is over and the applause overwhelms
the little microphone in the video camera. They bow.
Looking to an off-stage mentor, they bow again. From
our left, stage right, a man in a tuxedo walks onstage
carrying roses. To the florally hip observer it seems a
diva-sized bouquet. He hands them to the girl who just
sang for us.

She seems surprised, discomfited by the gift. Her
stage smile vanishes, replaced by the slightest hint of
worry. She looks around to her fellows. They are applauding, too, now, pointing their slapping hands at
her and smiling.

The red-headed girl looks to the camera, then down
at the roses. She reaches inside the paper, jiggles, pulls,
removes a rose and hands it to a boy beside her in the
front row. He head-shakes a refusal, she shoves an in-
sistence. He takes the rose and she goes down the line,
dividing her trophy among the singers.

When all the flowers are gone, she turns her back
to the camera and begins to applaud. We don't see
much of this since she is quickly lost to us in a sea of
hugging arms and laid-on hands.

1.

Paula, twenty-four years old, looks in a full-length mirror on the wall of a restaurant's cramped changing room. Shoulder-length red hair, freckles, black bow tie, white shirt, black skirt, workaday stockings and flat black shoes. She tickles her red hair out away from her face.

Paula is singing. Her voice is soft and wonderfully pure. The melody is motet, not mo'town. A song that a person sings just because she can. The voice is an enviable, make-a-deal-with-the-devil-to-have-it voice and there is something sad about it. A disquieting note, if you will. Her styling, her shaping of the words has a slightly pained edge to it, not the utter tragedy of a doomed operatic character, not the mocking self-knowledge of a blues singer, but the dangerously sharp, jaggedy edge of a well nourished disappointment. The words are in a foreign language and no one in the back room of the restaurant recognizes the tune.

She has a little more flesh than usual for a woman her age, not fat, just thick; no sharp curves, just solid gentle undulations. Widest, she reflects, at the hips.

The face looking back at Paula is more delicate than her body. It is a sun-shy, near-pretty face. Freckles and green eyes. An unbudge-ably friendly face. The face of a woman who keeps a book of people's birthdays, sends cards, is sad when her envelopes come back stamped 'address unknown.'

The muscles around her mouth seem to have lost something, some range of motion, the strength to reach out to hilarity or down to tears. There are the first puffy traces of emotional flabbiness, the beginnings of a permanent cringe.

Whatever song she's singing, what she feels is her feet, stinging, ex-panding and shrinking from a night's pile driving into an un-cushioned restaurant carpet. Each step fishing for tips, $84.75 in her creel. She thinks it's a lot because she thinks it's hers.

There's a hollow banging on the door behind her. Paula turns and her hair follows her like the swirl of a skirt. We hear a lightly nasal, breathy but not unpleasant voice.

"C'mon for God's sake, I'm ready to party."

Paula accepts 'to party' as an intransitive verb—one that takes no, needs no, object. She even knows what it means. It means for her 'to be part of,' to be sucked up, absorbed: to merge into the fibers of something: to put salve on the sunburn of separateness that scratches her like a wool sweater on bare skin. That it might mean 'to part from' is something she doesn't think about now.

The voice belongs to Tom, square-jawed but oddly delicate, pale, blue-gray eyes showing violet behind the tinted contact lenses. He is Paula's best girlfriend and he makes her laugh.

"Okayokayokay" and she flicks the hook that holds the door. Paula wants to party too.

Paula and Tom on the eleven-PM October street. The smells are leaves, wet pavement and motor oil. The rain has stopped, granting Paula permission to leave her folding rubber boots behind. Through thin-soled flat shoes, the cool wet of the pavement soothes her feet.

Paula rolls as she walks, Tom bounces. Paula's black trench coat brushes Tom's brown leather jacket. She stays well stuck to the earth, he disdains it. Lightly. After a few steps they are in rhythm. Urban army hup-two. They are talking softly, the brumble-sounds of their voices have a cuddly, intimate tone. Tom is telling Paula a funny story about last weekend, about how he took his little sister to the mall and how she begged him to buy her a bra because mom says she doesn't believe in breasts. Paula tells him about tomorrow's audition for a commercial for a car dealer. The producer is going to put a muscle car on the foredeck of a tugboat and he wants someone to sing 'Cruising Down the River' with Ella Fitzgerald styling. Tom pats her shoulder as they walk and he half sings, half talks 'There's no business like show business.'

Paula and Tom think they tell each other anything. They have permission to call in the sleeping hours, the intrusion being not so much a prerogative of friendship as its test. Look, I wake you up, you must love me. Tom is impatient with Paula's loneliness, but he helps it go away. He brings her close to sequins and fancy dancing. Paula reminds Tom of home; mashed potatoes and meat loaf. It's a deal.

Ahead of them, the edge of a neon sign in the middle of the block pokes finger-thick lines of red, blue and green. The three colors add up to a cone of light that is almost white. Paula thinks of a stage. In the light she sees three men and a woman. Paula knows them. They have common restaurants, lovers, roommates. As Paula and Tom approach, hands raise, faces smile, shoulders are patted. Everybody has tip money, everybody has fun.

Paula likes these people, the ones on the street and the ones in the bar. She inflates their virtues and prays for their hopes. She's diluted her affections and washed them over the whole tribe. She saves up the warmth that she can't give herself, gives it to them.

Tom turns sharply to the left, urgent words for the tall man at the edge of the group. They whisper, they laugh. Paula turns her back to them, says hellos again, folds her arms and smiles at the brown-haired woman.

Past the group on the sidewalk, down the street, at the corner, there's a traffic light on a pole. A man is standing hunched and jerking. He zips up a green satin team jacket, pulls at a soft black cap.

"Hi Paulie, sure is cold out here." The brunette bobs her head and turns toward a wooden door with four glass panes at eye height. Paula turns her face to the neon; it says Skipper's. The brunette flips her head at the two other men and they follow her. One of them pulls the brass stirrup door handle and the door opens and Paula hears the lonely sounds of bar music, glass crackles and well-mixed conversations. A few seconds later, she smells the warm-air beery smell of close bodies.

The man in the green jacket has left the safety of the traffic light. He's crossed the street, walking toward Paula, Tom and the tall man. His head is down, hands in his pockets, walking faster.

Paula turns back toward Tom. She takes a step, feeling clumsy inside, closer to Tom. The tall man winks at Tom, smiles at Paula, two steps, opens the door. Bar sounds leak out again. Tom moves to follow him, his arm out to Paula, wrapping her up and moving her with him.

"Hey, um," Paula slows, stops him. Eyes signaling a wait-a-minute. Tom fingerwiggles see-you-in-a-minute to the tall man, the door closes. She pulls Tom out of the light. She recognizes the flirting, the crotchy attraction between the two men. She's a little bit jealous—not of the tall man but of the ease with which they seem to have sealed a deal that she's always bumbled. She doesn't want to stop him, and she hates to let him go, so she settles for one more minute. Over the zipping of tires on wet pavement, she says "Who was that?"

The green-jacketed man is now fifteen yards away. His knitted black cap has unrolled to a ski mask over his face.

Paula, smiling, teasing, wanting some dish, wanting to hang on to Tom for a minute more. The man with the ski cap is a step away. If Paula were listening, she would hear the sucky smack of his sneakers on the concrete, hear the rhythm of his steps accelerate.

"Oh, you know him, that's—"

Then there's a grunt, a blow, the slap of clothes and the woof of Tom hitting the concrete.

Paula's face goes blank, then she opens her mouth to scream, but there's a gun hard against her face and no sound comes out. A stained beige leather glove holds her hair, pressing her face into the side of the gun. The gun is pointed up, its muzzle half under her left eyebrow. Her upper lip is pressed back, there's a spot of blood. The metal feels warm on her face and she thinks she tastes sweat. Tom is on the ground, face down, right leg pulled up, toes curled under like a sprinter ready to push off. A patch of bloody red and pink has grown on the back of his head.

The voice is tight, strangled, but the loudest human thing Paula has ever heard.

"Give me your wallet you little cocksucker or I blow her away."

She can smell his breath, feel the tooth of the gun against her cheek. "Please, I'm pregnant." She flicks her eyes toward Tom. She doesn't know, as she says it, where it came from, this wish-filled plea for mercy.

He pulls the gun away from her face, points it to her belly. She can see the gunman smiling through the slit in his ski mask. Tom is on his right side looking up toward Paula, his left hand is fumbling in his pocket for something. Paula's confused, expectant. In the movies, this is where Tom pulls out his own pistol and surgically finishes the gunman with a bullet to the right eye.

The bar door opens and Paula sees side-lit the face of the tall man, sees him open his mouth. His eyes go from languid to scared. Music and bar sounds burst out on the street from behind him.

Then there's a scream, the sounds of tavern panic, glasses dropping, the dull ring of falling barstools.

A bright blue-white beacon over the door turns on, bleaching the gunman's figure in the light. Paula hears electronic yodeling from the bar behind her: an amateur siren, a call for help, not an arrival sign of the help itself.

The people in the bar hear the shot. The brown-haired girl is screaming in siren rhythm. One of the boys with her is lying on the floor, a
dark circle already visible in the crotch of his tan pants. It is not a polite
movie pop. It crashes into them, bores into their ears. They hear it in
their teeth and neck bones. It probes them, discovers things, makes un-
popular diagnosis, disappears.

2.

Paula is sitting on the edge of her bed. Her eyes are puffed and red and she does not move. Her upper lip is swollen and scabbed over and there is a bruise, yellow blue black under her left eye. Her stillness fills the room. There is no tension in her stillness, no holding back, only a sense of life lacking. Paula is wearing a pinkish gray nightgown tight around her neck, loose on her body. The nightgown stops at her knees, her legs have crossed themselves at the ankles and her ankles have then wilted toward the floor. All she can feel of her body is its weight and the depression it makes in the mattress.

The room is dead. Paula may be dead too. The only visible force is gravity. Paula looks around—stereotype girl mess; magazine piles on floors, laundry on a dresser, a glass vase half-filled with amber water. There's a thirteen-inch TV set, some bottles that may be cologne. Between Paula and the dresser an interior door is half open. Past a wilted brassiere on the door knob, there's another small dark room and a second, sturdier door with multiple locks. The room smells of steam heat and stale breath. A small digital clock is showing 12:04 in white numbers. Paula has evidently slept till noon. No phone calls, no urgent knocks on the door, her friends have apparently absorbed the tragedy without her.

On the floor by the dresser, an orange cat sleeps on a towel. The cat opens her eyes at the creak of bedsprings, follows bare feet across the floor, turns her ears to the sound of running water. A light, hollow-core door closes.

A half hour later Paula, dressed but ill-composed in her black raincoat, pushes her way through a scarred exterior door. She descends the five steps that make up the stoop in front of row houses in northeastern cities and takes a second to look at Pine Street. She loves this neighborhood, she thinks of it sometimes as the place where she really grew up. Ginkgo trees, mostly leafless, line both sides of the three-lane street.

The scene is reddish-gray and brown, the colors of sparrows and moths, spotted with a handful of small brightly colored signs:

RENTING

FOR RENT

APARTMENT

Paula passes small shops, dog-walkers, a wrinkled man glazed with dirt pushing a grocery cart. She passes a line of brown and bronze little girls, second grade she guesses. There are thirty of them in blue and white tartan skirts waiting at the corner. They are being nudged into some un-childlike line by a short, intense woman in a windbreaker. Paula's heart aches for them, for their innocence for fear that they might one day see the man in the windbreaker with the gun. She slows, she stares. One of the girls, a bit taller than the rest, notices Paula. Maybe she divines something in the wounded white girl: she waves her hand side to side and smiles at Paula and mouths 'hello.' Paula smiles back and then makes her fist into a puppet face that mouths hello back. The girl laughs and then a whistle blows and the kids are hurried across the street. The tall girl looks back once at Paula and then the line of blue and white tartan is gone.

On the broom-clean shabby street, there are other pedestrians, all of them in their twenties, all of them walking slowly. Paula's eyes look up above the two- and three-story shop front brick buildings, through some high-rise glass slabs. She sees a thin limestone tower with a bronze statue on top. The figure in bronze is oddly gentle for a municipal sculpture. If she could see it at eye level, the face would seem not to command but to beg. It's the face of the Quaker, William Penn.

A few minutes later, Paula is staring at another face, one with the shape and something of the color of an unripe beefsteak tomato. He is chanting, "The court will come to order, the court will come to order." She hears a very young woman's voice saying "tom-tom no, tom-tom noooo..."

The gunman, green jacket, black ski mask pulled down, is sitting at a table framed by the suited arms of men on either side of him. Paula imagines him bleached white, the way she saw him in front of the other bar. Paula hears her self saying "yes that's him over there," and her voice seems to echo 'him over there him over there overthere there there.' And what she's seeing is the line of little girls, all in blue and white.

Outside, there's a TV camera. Two small clusters of people are waiting, framing the doors from the courtroom. On Paula's right, they rally around a cardboard sign—a pink triangle outlined in red. There's a drawing of a handgun in the center of the triangle and a red bar through the handgun. On her left, another group is chanting "ARM GAYS! ARM GAYS! ARM GAYS!" One TV camera drifts to an upraised fist and then dawdles its way down to the shoulder. Arm gaze.

Paula is twisting her way between the demonstrators. The crowd is turned like a field of sunflowers to the TV cameras. Competing signs joust for position, there's a scuffle involving a bullhorn battery.

Paula is blocked by a man carrying a TV camera. He is attached by wire to a beautiful olive-tan, shiny-black-haired woman with a microphone. Her beauty arrests Paula. The camera zooms in and heads fill the screen, Paula full-faced on the left, the beauty in profile, cafe latte skin all Aztecs and Spaniards, on the right.

"Paula, Laura Garcia-Lane from channel 3. In court, you just confronted a man who had a gun to your face. How did that feel?"

Paula's eyes dart left, out of the frame. She wants to leave, feels commanded to stay. Her eyes focus on the microphone and she remembers the question. Then her eyes go slack and something inside her is visibly untied, drifting loose.

"Oh Tom, poor Tom . . . he loved courtroom drama . . . he . . ."

"What do you have to say to the demonstrators here?"

"I only wish that they had known him." Paula seems to be gulping air.

"What's your opinion about guns?"

"I don't know . . . I hate that gun . . . no, I don't know. I don't care about the guns . . . I care, I cared about Tom . . . it wasn't . . . oh, the gun. I don't know, it was that creepy man . . . oh God."

Paula lowers her head, turns left and half stumbles out of the frame. Laura Garcia-Lane says, "Back to you, Ralph." Paula runs through the crowd, slowing as she reaches its edge. The rhythm of Paula's steps quickly matches the pedestrians'. Pace-camouflaged, she disappears into the street.

Paula's letter home:

Dear Mom & Dad,

Thank you for coming down to see me—I've been very lonely and it was good to see your faces.

I'm feeling better now, but I still think about Tom all the time. I think about his little sister too, the one who looked up to him so much. I keep thinking about how he wanted to make such a big difference in her life and now he won't get to. She won't even know what she missed.

I've been thinking about what you said, about how Catsbody and I should move back home and about the job in DeWitt. I don't think I can do it. Please don't be angry with me. I really appreciate it and I really really miss you a lot, but I just can't.

I don't want to disappoint you, but I still think Philadelphia is the right place for me even if I can't say just why. I know you're scared for me and I guess I'm scared too. I just feel like maybe it's time to be brave.

I love you and I miss you. Please say hello to Aunt Mimi and tell Billy I'll write to him soon.

xxoo,
P.

3.

A week after Tom's funeral, Paula moves heavily through an evening of restaurant noises, sodawaterbottle conversations and cutlery clankles. As she works, she has little moments of brilliantly clear sensation. She sees the rubies in the bright red veins of a leaf of ruby chard. She jerks away from the prickly smell of saffron and marvels at the order she finds in aspirin-sized chunks of carrot and celery sprinkled on the rim of a plate. She sometimes notices a deadness in her gut or an ache along her jawline as if she had to scream but can't. At the end of her shift, she finds herself standing on the street looking at the front window of her restaurant, staring at the ocher drapes and the gold leaf letters that spell out Odetta. Inside, the lights are turned up and a man in a loose-fitted suit is vacuuming the floor. After a minute or two, she thinks of her cat and, being grateful for a reason to leave, turns away from the restaurant and heads for home.

The night is mild and she's carrying her coat. The street seems to have inhaled a lung full of servers from a dozen bistros. There is a person waving and talking to the south while walking unsteadily north. They all seem to be drifting, bouncing off each other in Brownian motion. They are ready to be blown home or into places like Skipper's, which is down the street on the right.

In the cone of light again, the sidewalk is crowded tonight, the warm street sucking customers out of saloons. A woman, small, brunette and perky pops out of the mass and bounces up to Paula. She is wearing a black sweatshirt with the Letters D R E X E L in an arc across her bosom. She remembers just in time to put her smile away. "Hi Paulie, did you hear about Tom?"

Paula starts to speak, starts, perhaps, to explain herself, to claim her rightful share in the tragedy. She is standing a few inches from the pock that the bullet left in the pavement. She sees the tall man with three others around him. His head is down, his eyebrows pressed together to say 'sensitive man in pain.' He is being touched and stroked in the manner of ants meeting their nest-mates on the trail.

The perky brunette is looking at Paula, she knows that she has done something clumsy, hates the feeling. Only the really dorky girls in college ever did things like that and none of them were in her sorority. She calls this awkward feeling an illegal alien, wants to deport it to Paula, doesn't dare, could make things worse. Frozen in place. Paula stares at the tall man, no one else is looking at her. Paula is going black inside, leaving, coming back. Returns to the scene of the crime. Five or six seconds have passed. Looking over the brunette's shoulder, Paula's face grows a touch of life, one raised eyebrow even suggests humor. "Yeah, I heard it loud and clear," and she ducks a shoulder as if she were going to crawl under the brunette, says "G'night," and heads down the street with her arms hugging themselves and her coat across her chest.

Until Now, Tom and Paula had all their wounds in common. Every hurt was diluted immediately, reduced by half for being shared, reduced again, almost redeemed by the attention that it earned. This pain though, is not some paradoxical currency that she can trade for love. Paula has been ambushed again in front of Skipper's.

Paula climbs her stoop. A minute later she's shuffling through her living room, crossing a pool of pink light that's come in from the streetlamp. She walks quietly, sneaking in her own apartment. The squeals of the floorboards seem suddenly ominous and for an instant she is afraid of the shadows. She sheds the outdoors with thumps and slaps and the dull music of hangers in a closet. Paula comes in to the bedroom and the bra on the doorknob swings as she pushes the door aside. She tries to sing as she kicks off her shoes, to blow the day out of her throat with a scale or a trill, but something seems to choke her off.

In a minute, Paula in pink chenille, is leaning with one hand on the dresser, turning on the TV, spinning a knob with gentle, almost affectionate strokes. She seems to be greeting it, not adjusting it. Television will keep her company, she thinks, as the picture brightens. Paula has turned on the news, she rubs her hands together and almost smiles. This newscaster, this graying, solid man whose face she can barely see on the snowy screen, is her imaginary playmate. They are about to spend some time alone.

Paula joins the news as it opens with the nightly fire. This one's a minor-leaguer in Kensington, the camera hangs on a smoldering mattress, lingers. Usually she warms her hands by the house fire story, but tonight she fiddles with the knobs, then settles back, two pillows holding her up in bed. Her friend says he'll be right back and we cut to commercial: a man in a dark suit, maybe forty years old, is standing in a park. There are trees overhead and cannon on spindly wheels in the background. The man's voice is earnest and soothing, like a veterinarian telling us our dog needs surgery but everything will be all right.

"Hello, I'm Senator Jim Santacci speaking to you from Valley Forge where the privately owned guns of American patriots won us the freedoms that we enjoy today. My opponent in this election wants to take guns away from the citizens of Pennsylvania. He says that being un-armed will protect us from criminals. Maybe we should ask the victims of crime what they think."

Cut to a black and white still photo of Paula, a frame from this morning's video tape. The photo floats in the center of the screen surrounded by black. Paula's voice saying "It wasn't the gun, it was that man."

Paula pushes herself out of bed. She snaps off the television, takes two steps toward the window and pulls down the shade. In the almost total darkness, two more steps and a bed creaking. There's a sharp, rattling sound like someone shivering and then some croaking hurt-animal noises. Paula is sobbing or gasping for breath in the dark.

4.

Morning. Silence. There's a round pedestal table next to the head of the bed and a telephone on it. Paula sits on the edge of the bed, nodding and writing something down, dialing, yawning, scratching her left side. She is not freshly awake, but has just decided to give up on sleep. The room is colder than it was last night, its scent fainter. Paula takes two steps to a case on her dresser and runs her fingers down the spines of the cassette tapes. She pulls out a tape marked Christmas Music, School Cor. and then slides it back. She hesitates over Scol Cant.: Verdi and Gergassingen, then settles for one marked: DAD-New piano!! The music starts in the middle of a piece as she reaches for the phone. She dials and hears the ringing as if she were inside it.

"Re-elect Santacci."

"Hello, I'd like to speak to whoever does your advertising." Choking on exhausted anger, her voice scrapes its way out of her throat.

"I'm sorry, no one from media is here right now, can I take a message?"

"Well, not really, I wanted to find out about that ad you ran last night, the one about the guns."

"I didn't see that, why don't I switch you over to voice mail?"

"No, I don't want—"

"Hello, you've reached the office of the Campaign Coordinator for Senator Santacci. To use your credit card to make a contribution to the Senator's campaign, press one now. To volunteer for the campaign, press two. For help with voter registration, press three. To speak to campaign staff, press four and to leave a message for the Senator, press five. To return to this menu at any time, press the star key."

Paula's right index finger advances to the dial and hesitates between 4 and 5. The finger looks chewed or torn around the cuticle and in the putrid cold light, the wounds look monstrous. She touches 4.

Paula's fingers work the handset, choking it, arousing it, begging it.

She feels her breath between each ring. Two rings, four rings. Paula listens, then following cues, pokes the dial again. The star key and then the 5. The tones in sequence remind her of something and she presses them again. The interval between them is a minor third and it calls to mind a lullaby. She shifts herself backwards on her bed, covers her mouth with her right hand in a polite throat clearing gesture, but the only sound in the morning room is the ringing.

"Hello, this is Senator Jim Santacci. I'm sorry that I can't answer your call right now, but I really want to hear from you and from every Pennsylvanian. Please leave a message at the sound of the tone and I'll see that someone gets back to you to address your concern. Leave your name, address and telephone number and we'll get back to you. That's a promise. This is Jim Santacci and I listen to you."

Paula's face has softened, her grip is relaxed on the handset.

"Senator Santacci, my name is Paula Sherman. I'm the woman whose picture you used . . . in your ad? the one about the guns?" Paula is losing herself in rising inflections. Outraged virtue doesn't have question marks. She shakes her head 'no.'

"I just want you to know that I didn't say what you made it sound like I said, and I think it's really horrible of you to . . . to do that and. . ." Her voice is failing her. "I want you to stop. If you don't I'm going to tell everybody what you did." Then, remembering her instructions: "This is Paula Sherman and my address is 1706 Pine Street, Philadelphia one nine one four six."

Then, remembering other instructions from her mother about giving out her phone number, Paula hangs up. She is a perfectly swirled frozen dessert, layers of creamy fatigue and ice-crystal anger wrapping around each other. Awash in mutual antidotes, she pounds her fist weakly on the round table. The sound is thin, almost hollow in the chilly bedroom.

5.

Several days have passed. Paula, in the changing room, is reading from a sheet of paper.

"I thank you for your interest in my campaign for re-election, if there's anything else I can do. . ." One woman, lean, small-eyed, ski jump nose, giggles to please, guesses at her own misreading, blushes, looks down and away. The other, thirtyish and thick, hears the hurt and hugs Paula, kisses her on the cheek. Paula's head draws back, takes aim, eyes half closed. Their lips stretch toward a common center and they hear the shuffle of feet and a boisterous "god what a night" from somewhere and the faces turn to buddy smiles. Look to their hands, skin stretched tight in squeezing.

Later, in her bedroom, Paula, glistening hair wet and brushed, comes out of the bathroom door. She goes, naked, to her cassette case and finds a tape marked EDWARD. It's violin music and it promises in the first few bars something edgy and weird. She pulls a pale t-shirt down over her belly, then steps into loosely fitting underpants. She climbs forward, crawls over the bed toward the window and then turns to the left. She settles with a groan on her back. Her hands and feet push the covers from underneath her and she rolls her shoulders into the pillows. She makes a tiny moan, so strained that it is almost spoken.

Paula's hands, which had been supporting her arched back, come to attention at the hem of the t-shirt. She gathers a handful of hem and saws it leftright across her thighs. Another handful, hemwad thicker, she fiddles on her pubis, rapid grabbing motions, stretching tension. Paula is controlling a thick hardened rod of cotton just underneath her breasts. Stretching it, she presses it down into her ribs and then up toward her chin. The roll of cloth compresses her breasts into her chest and draws them up to her chin. It snaps roughly over her nipples, slightly mismatched promontories on half dollar sized aureoles. Then Paula pushes the roll back toward her knees with a sawing motion that first flattens her breasts and then stretches her nipples downward. When she lets the hemroll snap over the rise of her nipples, she reverses direction. She bowsaws her breasts, popslapping them with the shirt and rocking her torso against the motion of her hands.

The movement ends, t-shirt thrown up like a used rag, Paula's hands go to her breasts, thumb on top, index finger below the nipple, squeeze, stretch down toward her crotch, her hands slipping and digging at the insides of her thighs, forcing the flesh and the cloth of her crotch into a pressed mound. Her fingers slide under the cloth, a tiny wet squawk of Paula finding herself, and then she is alone in the dark and some thumping strings playing. Pizzicato.

6.

December. Paula is leaving Odetta. There is a dusting of snow on the ground and a few flakes are sawing their way softly through the air. Paula is wearing a black beret to go with her trench coat. Her red hair is a shocking display on the almost monochrome street. Someone leaving with her has handed her a magazine with a yellow cover.

Paula flips the pages, and as she walks, she finds it. It's a two-page spread in black and white. On the right-hand page is the same shot of Paula that she saw on the TV screen. Paula closes the magazine and rolls it and tapping against her thigh, walks home.

Between the windows in her sitting room, there's a sofa covered in leeridescent pink and green. The coat, the magazine and Paula all end up there in one lumpy let-go gesture. She unrolls the magazine: TELESCOPIC SIGHT DIGEST subtitled The Magazine of Death from a Distance. The cover illustration is a long-barreled pistol. Except for a black checkered grip, the pistol is all stainless steel. In case we miss the luster, there are several starbursts drawn in on the barrel and trigger guard. The weapon is pointed safely at a spot above the reader's left shoulder. Mounted on top like a panther on a wildebeest is a green contraption with lots of slots and screws. She expects to see the stainless bleed from the claw marks. On top of the green thing is a black tube with a ruby-coated lens. Paula's fingers reach out to the picture then pull back.

The magazine opens itself to Paula's picture. It is three and a half inches tall and two and a half inches wide, just above center. The size of a playing card. Queen of what? The rest of the page is black except for some feminine handwriting in white that reads, "It wasn't the gun, it was that man." On the facing page, also reversed against the black, is bold type: *Crime Victims Speak Out*

There's more, there's text, there's an 800 number, there's the logo of the United Gun Association, but Paula closes the magazine. And then she opens it again, turning the cover back to the double-page truck ad, then to the Table of Contents and the ad for the limited edition titanium Colt .44.

". . . its critical feature, incredible hardness!"

Paula has been had. Suckered. Used. Frattyboy prank, guess who's got the red ass? She knows that mixture of shame and centrality. Goon show star makes 'em laugh. She wants to puke with hatred of her stupid self; she wants to call home to say she got her picture in a magazine.

She flips a few more pages. The president of the United Gun Association died. It doesn't say how he died, but he looks fat and young and shiny in the photo. Maybe he was blown away like Tom, pieces of his lung bouncing up from the pavement back into his chest. Or, maybe not. Paula is slowed and sad. Right below the obit is the news that Sagittarius Arms has resurrected the model 85. Paula is pleased. She likes the sound of the word 'resurrect.'

Another flip. A model-gorgeous Teutonic blonde with ear protectors and safety glasses is firing a pistol off to our left. No need to duck. Below her are photos of strange machines with levers and model numbers all their own. Paula turns the page past What's New, past an ad for the Warrior Swords of the Samurai. A Column called Second Amendment mentions Paula by name. It praises her for 'cutting to the nitty-gritty of the guns and crime thing.'

Paula feels a buzz as she reads the piece and flips the page. Her movement is waxy and automatic, she is too numb to cringe as the pages smack her, tickle her, touch her. The magazine is reading Paula. The next column is called Line of Fire. Its author is Rachel Sam Hicock and her photo is there by her byline. Another blonde; commanding, black clad and sporting an enormous handgun in a holster that starts at her waist and ends just below her breast.

Paula is stirred and reassured; if Rachel had been in front of Skipper's that night if Paula were Rachel if Rachel were here now she would make Paula feel better. Better feel.

Paula has seen enough movies about English women in India to know what it means to swoon. She closes the magazine before she does, spirals her way up from the couch and walks it in front of her into her bedroom. She sets TELESCOPIC SIGHT DIGEST on her night table using both hands.

In spite of her near-faint, it will be a long time before Paula sleeps.

In bed, lights out, the room will spin like a pot of briskly stirred soup. In the dark, little bits of ideas and images will pop out of Paula and coagulate. Images of Tom twice-killed; her father, short and potbellied, throwing himself between her and a neighbor's vicious dog; a scene from a movie where the heroine is beaten by her boyfriend. Ideas. They can't do that to me. They did. An egg drop nebula of teeth-grinding rage. It will keep Paula company through the night, light her up, make her glow. She would sing to it if she could, but she can't. Voiceless since Tom died.

Just before dawn, she howls once. She doesn't even wonder if the neighbors heard. She squeezes grunts and moans out against clenched teeth, locked jaw. Her fists pound the bed. She thinks she's dying and quite the opposite will be true.

7.

"Good Morning, Channel Three, the People's Choice, How may I direct your call?"

"Newsroom please." The second voice is Paula's, her words are precise and rehearsed.

"Newsroom." This voice is male, abrupt.

"Laura Garcia Lane, please"

Clickbeep

"Production."

"Laura Garcia Lane, please"

"Yeah, wait a minute. . ."

"This is Laura Garcia Lane."

Paula is sitting on the edge of her bed, her eyes turned toward the window light. She is wearing jeans, a white button-down collar shirt and horizontally striped socks of blue and gold. Her feet slide and tap their way around the faded green carpet as she talks.

"Miss Garcia Lane? Hi. My name is Paula Sherman, I'm sure you don't remember me, but you interviewed me outside City Hall last month. My friend was killed in a mugging and I was a witness and I had to. . ."

"Paula. Yes, Paula, I do remember you. I remember thinking that I'd kill to have that fabulous red hair . . . umm . . . but that's not why I remember you. God, that was a shitty thing that happened. How are you?"

Paula is put off, spun around, her whole identification speech short-circuited.

"I'm fine—no, not fine. . ." She sees, in half-hallucination, Laura interviewing her, then the Santacci commercial, then the magazine spread.

Laura is sitting in a swivel chair inside a green-walled box. She turns herself from side to side, moving papers on her walls as she goes, nodding as she listens. The cubicle is small and she can touch opposite walls without leaving her chair.

Over Laura's shoulder on the green wall is a picture of St. Clare, the patron saint of television. Like Paula, St. Clare is in bed with her face turned to a glowing light. Laura speaks.

"Those fucking sons of bitches!" She pronounces the 'g.' She is not screaming, her voice is a breathy roar, high intensity, low volume, passion-in-a-cubicle whisper . "They can't fucking do that to you! Ohmigod, we'll stop them. We'll, umm, the station owns the copyright on that tape, we've got lawyers, we'll sue their balls off."

Paula freezes, speechless with joy, in love with Laura's fury even more than she prizes her agreement.

"Listen Paula, I can't really talk now, can you meet me for a drink after work? Good. No, not around here. *Eponymous Doc's?* About two thirty, okay?

Paula and Laura at a cocktail table, their necks bent forward, heads a hand's distance apart. On the tiny white tiles of the floor, shadow letters read '. . . ous Doc's.' Paula does the talking, gesturing with her palm up. Her hand is wondrously white against the brown table top. Laura is nodding, writing.

Paula pays for drinks, they leave. Their unbuttoned coats flap in the wind. A few minutes later, in Paula's front room. Paula, eyes wet, is showing Laura her mementos of Tom, pointing to magazine spreads. Even with the light coming over their shoulders and flaring on the lens, we recognize the black and white UGA ads.

Laura picks up, then puts down one of Paula's gun magazines. Her voice is nasal and thin, like someone who's about to vomit. "Boys" she says. "Boys and their stupid little bang-bangs."

Ten A.M. The morning story conference at KYJ-TV is meeting around a U-shaped table. The open end faces a video screen. When the station was remodeled, this room was described as a State-of-the-Art News Communication and Decision-Making Facility. Story ideas were to be made up on a computerized story board program and projected on the screen. But the news director couldn't figure out how to use the system and nobody wanted to embarrass him. So Laura is waiting her turn, down at the screen end of the table with a flip pad pasted up with images and text.

Her story flips by. It's called "A Stolen Life" and it looks a little like the montage version that Paula runs in her head. Paula is described as "an aspiring concert singer." Tom becomes simply "the man she loved." There's footage from the trial, a flash of a campaign ad. Laura's voice sounds urgent, sentimental. It's a story to cry for, a story to forget.

We hear a man's voice, tired and impatient. "All right, you get two minutes: next Tuesday on the six o'clock."

Back to Doc's, girls at the bar, Paula and Laura laughing. Paula throws a bill on the bar, finger-signals the barkeep for 'two.' Hands are squeezed. Laura is talking, hands and lips moving quickly. Paula is nodding to every fourth beat; as her smile fades slowly, her eyes focus on something off in the distance and we go to black.

8.

Paula's brain has become a flip book full of gun images. Paula, who had never really noticed guns before, now sees them everywhere. They are her magnetic north, her allergy. She dowses them like a water witch, quivering as she comes near them. She senses guns behind closed doors, through bank vault walls. Her eyes linger on the holsters of cops. She watches a Brinks truck moving cash into a hamburger joint and studies the small pistol worn high above the belt of the guard who pushes the hand truck full of pennies. The magazine rack at Borders bookstore flashes the words at her—BAM! POP! ZOW! The jackets of mysteries, the poster for a movie comedy, a toy display in a dusted-over antique store window.

She finds herself searching the bumpers and back windows of parked cars. She finds herself finding. United Gun Association decals remind her of Masonic emblems in lapels. Hey, whattya packin', Hiram?

If only she had a gun that night, if only she had one now.

It is the UGA decals floating on the glass over the dark interiors of suburban military utility vehicles that bother her the most; ugly insect eyes searching for victims, black and gold windshield rectums pouring guns on her street. Why are these cars in the city? What could a four-wheel drive station wagon land Wehrmacht-mobile be doing in the city except carrying guns and death and Tom, oh, Tom.

When Tom was alive, he teased her, poked her, pecked at all her illusions. And he loved her singing, went to church to hear her solos, dragged out of bed to sit with her before auditions. In Tom's world, she was a diva, a voice. If nothing else was very good, no excitement, no sex, no money, no fun, there was always Tom and the dream of the music. And now she's alone. There is no Tom, and in his place there's a swarm of stinging, biting guns.

A nightmare, Paula thinks, is when your reality gets flayed off of you and another reality is dabbed on with insect precision and dries and hardens and encases you like a Thompson's turkey. So every walk to work, every trip to the grocery store is her little nightmare. She would like to shove the nightmare to the sidewalk, shoot it once in the chest, watch it die.

Paula has her consolations too. She will have her moment on the six o'clock news. She asked for Tuesday night off. She's told her friends, Tom's friends, everybody.

At night, in her flannies, with her cat, she pages back to front through TELESCOPIC SIGHT DIGEST. She has added a few titles to her collection, picking up copies of magazines that ran the ad with her face. She opens one or two of them a night, turns each pages slowly, deliberating on the hidden meanings. The articles about guns make her dizzy, she patches together some meaning from the strange words and reads them anyway. She submerges herself in the articles about shooting, imagining herself 'blasting away at the 25-yard bench with this brand spankin' new smoke wagon.' Her shot-groups, she knows, are tight and in the black.

She listens to a tape whose case bears the single word Leider. The voice on it is her own and some of the songs sound pitiful and some of the songs sound heroic. She sometimes finds herself touching the speakers on the small black one-piece stereo. In the steam on her bathroom mirror she has finger painted: THE STRONG BELONG and her nights are much much easier than her days.

9.

There is a two-top just inside the window at Odetta. The maitre d' tries to keep that table filled so that the restaurant looks busy from the street. If he can seat an attractive pair there, he's pleased. If they are desperately fashionable, he is happy. Someday he hopes to find a milk-white pair of androgynes dressed in skintight metallic jumpsuits, each stroking their own shoulder-mounted iguanas and drinking something blue from martini glasses.

Tonight, just after opening, he doesn't know how he feels. The Center Stage twotop is occupied by two men, a pair, not a couple. Looking from inside the restaurant, the man on the right is engaging in a dark and dangly sort of way: six feet tall with an excess of arms and legs, curly black hair and lightly olive skin on a broad open face. His black suit and turtle neck are clerical sensual. Clothes for an ascetic tap dancer. He seems to be completely free from guile and artifice; a monk, a rabbi, a man just emerged from a six-year coma, a Jesuit, a simpleton, an assassin.

The other's feet have to point to touch the carpet. He is not exactly a trophy dwarf, but he has an earthen solidity about him. You could imagine him swinging, in a few compact movements, down a manhole to his home beneath the streets. Maybe he was in a fairy tale that the maitre d' heard once. He is wearing a dark blue pin-striped suit. His white French cuffs are held in place by a subtle Turk's head knot of gold.

They have their salads, there's a bottle of Penfold's Bin 707 on the table. The dwarf is talking between bites of radicchio and star fruit and his companion, who hasn't picked up a fork, is making notes on a green spiral-bound steno pad. He is not, we see immediately, taking dictation. In fact he is only formally aware of the small man. He is taking notes on something else, yes, on something that no one else sees.

Paula knows him, he is her neighbor, 1700 Pine 4th Floor. She has seen him sitting on the stoop holding his cat and drinking exotic beer from the bottle. The beer, she thinks, is a pose. The cat is not. That is love. She could tell from the rolling motion of his thumb and forefinger on the cat's loose fur and the intensely present look in his eyes as he stroked her.

What Paula doesn't know is that his name is Emanuel Cardoso, he is a food writer for a weekly giveaway newspaper and a sometime wine teacher. He is thirty-seven years old. The short man is Harvey Lichtmann, fifty-one years old, assistant counselor to the City Council. Hobby: malicious gossip, low-stakes blackmail. Lichtmann's ears are tiny and the skin at the top seems to fold into a point. Paula thinks she has seen him on a fresco somewhere.

Paula is bringing Cardoso a pair of cruets, oil and vinegar. As she lowers the vinegar cruet, she has a vision.

Cardoso in his chair is naked. Paula removes the stopper from the oil cruet and pours the oil slowly on his head. Cardoso tilts his chin up, and as the oil runs down his back, Paula massages it into his skin. His skin absorbs the oil completely, graciously, thankfully.

She recognizes the vision as the return of her favorite romantic fantasy, the one about the perfect gift accepted perfectly.

There is a main course. Paula lays down a plate of lobster medallions in an orange vinegar sauce and another with a pylon of tuna, rare, with lacy thin fried potatoes whirled into a nest on top. Streaks of wasabi and mustard cream crisscross the plate underneath the tuna. As she turns away from the table, Lichtmann is slicing off a piece of his tuna and handing it, on a bread plate, to Cardoso. His gesture recalls a surgeon passing a length of artery. They are trading information, not nourishment.

Paula outside, stealthy-walking in the shadows, looking up and down the street before she unlocks her door. A few minutes later, she's in bed with her magazine. Her eyes are sharp, squeezed like someone squinting for distance. She pulls each page across from right to left, keeping her grip low and close to the book. She will surprise something in there. Her cat is standing at Paula's shoulder, eyes focused on the page just where Paula's are. Her tail is twitching, tapping out the meter of excitement. She sees a small ad with the headline: SILENT, LEGAL, LETHAL. Paula's eyes widen and then narrow again. Her right hand goes to the bed table, paper, penclick, tiniest perceptible smile, write, fold, envelope, stamp and darkness. The cat sitting in the light from the window has focused on something outside, her tail still twitching the predator beat.

10.

Nobody could get away to join her for the news, and Paula and Catsbody are alone. She ejects a tape from her stereo and carefully puts it in a box marked State Chorus. The tape is back in its case as she switches on the TV set.

"Good evening and welcome to the six o'clock edition of Phillynews, I'm Rod Vaigh. Tonight's lead story takes us to the town of Milton in Berks County, Pennsylvania where four students are dead and eleven injured after two high school students staged a wild west-style gun fight in a crowded cafeteria. We'll be showing you an exclusive animated re-enactment of today's tragedy right after these messages."

After commercial, Rod narrates the cartoon version of today's top shooting. Inside a sketchily drawn low-ceilinged room, he pans along lines of tables packed with kids. There is no sound track, but the children seem quiet, heads bobbing over their lunches like the hungry little animated figures they are. At one end of the room, three boys in long, black duster coats are talking. They are pulled up tight to each other: a huddle of three. The tallest boy breaks the huddle and steps toward the middle of the room. He seems to be shouting. A cut to the other side shows four younger boys slouching in loose-fitting denims. Rod tells us that they are a school gang; the Erps. The older three are the Glands. All are members of the school gun club.

The shout seems to have galvanized the Erps. One of the boys shrugs off his jacket, unsnaps the clip on his overalls and lets them fall to the ground. Beneath the blues, he is wearing track shorts and a short-barreled carbine. He fiddles with a catch, raises the stock to his shoulder and with the coveralls still around his ankles, begins firing across the room in the general direction of the Erps.

The animator backs off and we see the whole cafeteria at once. The Erps return the fire, one of them using two pistols at once. Each bullet's flight is traced in red on the screen, Rod counts off the hits on human flesh. Onetwothree, four, five, sixseveneight. Nine, ten. Eleven.

Paula's eyes are as red as the bullet traces. She is shuddering to no particular rhythm, little seismic jerks and spasms rocking her as the announcer's voice goes on.

"The gunfight was apparently pre-arranged between the two rival groups. Originally scheduled for Monday, it was postponed for a day because one of the boys had band practice."

Paula continues to flinch as if she is herself being hit by tiny bullets. A new announcer is interviewing Roscoe 'Bepp' Baxter, congressman from Alabama. ". . . solution is for teachers themselves to be armed. Over one hundred unanswered shots were fired in that cafeteria, and a single armed teacher could have stopped that fight. In fact just knowing that there were armed, law-abiding citizens would have been enough to prevent this tragedy."

Paula's grief is turning, fermenting, case hardening. Her breaths are longer and slower. Her lower lip, that quivered through the story of the shootout, is pulled back. She is trembling from her chest out to her clenched fists.

She almost doesn't care that her story didn't run and she turns off the set and her vision is erased as the TV screen turns to a Rothko rectangle of red and black. It's a shape and a color that reminds her of rage.

11.

Most days, the UPS truck, brown and square, hits the 1700 Block of Pine Street around 11 o'clock. Paula has taken to watching for it. From her window, she can see for more than a block, well down into the 1800s. She notices the frequent stop at the antiques dealer, another every day at the picture framer. She has added up all the unreturned phone calls and concluded that Laura and her station were not interested in suing the UGA over a few seconds of tape. She is starting to think that Laura was using her and Tom just as much as the Santacci campaign was.

Today, it's 11:26 when the truck stops in front of her house. She is on her way down the stairs before the bell rings. The driver is a young blonde woman with old brunette eyebrows. The package in her hand is nine by eighteen inches, maybe three inches thick. The word TEMPEST is stenciled across its face and it has no readable return address.

Paula carries the package in front of her as she walks back up the stairs, she makes little curling motions, enjoying its weight, glad for the gravity. She's excited, she's scared and she knows that nothing will ever be the same again.

Cardoso's Diary 1

My name is Emanuel Cardoso and I have become, thanks to a set of circumstances and predilections too bizarre to mention, a man whose ruling passions and personal madness have been stripped away. With the core of my craziness gone, a great deal else is gone too. I find myself almost completely without lusts and cravings. It would not be too much to say that I barely have preferences. I have a few consistencies, almost enough to give me what may be thought of as a personality, but my most compelling characteristic right now is my almost total emptiness; a blankness that's not like the desolation of winter but closer to the expectant vacancy of early spring.

Curiously, the blankness of my slate does not seem to compel the people with whom I come in contact to take up chalk and scratch themselves upon me. On the contrary, they seem eager, even desperate that I inscribe something on them. That I have little to say about their concerns and speak mostly of the obvious does not seem to deter a stream of acquaintances from seeking my company and advice.

I would tell you here the story of my personal transformation if I thought that there were the slightest chance that you could emulate it or find the emulation of the slightest use. It is a story of obsession and rage, loathsome occurrences and a very close acquaintance with death. So much of my story seems to turn on happenstance, that I can't imagine anyone finding either comfort or instruction in it. Telling the story of how I became this vacant sage would be nothing more than a treat for my ego. Since I have scarcely any ego to treat, I will ask you to accept my present condition as the axiom of my story and hear me out.

Once a week or so, I climb from my fourth-floor apartment to the roof of my building and sit, balanced at the edge of the roof and watch the street below me. I sit for an hour or so and I sometimes bring a small thermos of tea. My building is on a corner, and I have a privileged view of an urban intersection with two pinkish street lights. I fancy myself in some kind of meditation.

Most nights the corner of 17th and Pine Streets in Philadelphia is a souk for one to three male prostitutes. Most of them come from the white working class neighborhood just to the south. They are very young and I am told that, in spite of having sexual congress with half a dozen men every night, most of them do not consider themselves homosexual.

I have been almost without sexual urges for some time and my interest in the scene below me is mostly a matter of marksmanship. My practice is to imagine inside my self a bolus of benevolence, a perfect sphere of good will. I am not always able. On nights when I can create a baseball-size piece, I imagine it floating from my gut, up through my chest, down my arm and into my hand. I imagine my fingers across the seams. I see a short windup and a snap throw down on the boy whores or their customers or the neighbors who pass unknowing through the pools of the light on their way home.

Last night, just before midnight, I watched a boy bobbing from car to car in the cold. He was underdressed for the weather and I tried to imagine warming him with my thoughts. The effort left me shocked at my own vanity. When he jumped into a car that stopped to chat him up, I was relieved for us both and turned my attention away from his corner. I could see, coming toward me on 17th Street, a coated figure. As she walked into the street light, I could see her bright red hair and the rough texture of the web belt on the bag worn like a bandoleer cross-chest. I recognized her as a neighbor. She lives, I think, at 1706 or 8 and works front-of-the-house at Odetta. She has waited on me there, most recently when I went to write a review of it. I see her from time to time when the cat and I are taking the air on our stoop.

I was struck by her unusual walk. She was walking against the one-way flow of traffic. She takes sixseveneight paces and then turns to peer at the rear of the parked car she has just passed. I have a flash of kid memory and I guess that she's playing license plate bingo and needs a 'Z' or a 'Q' before she reaches Pine Street. I was rooting for her. Just before she reached the corner, I saw her double check the rear of a Jeep Wagoneer. It was not the license plate but something on the rear window that caught her attention. She put her right hand deep in her shoulder bag and stepped off the curb into the space between the Jeep and the car parked behind it. She thrust the bag toward the Jeep's window, I heard a whoosh and a crack, I saw her step back on the pavement and continue walking toward the corner. She did not stop to check any more cars. A minute later, she crossed Pine and disappeared from my sight.

I returned to my apartment puzzled. This seemed like a very small-hearted kid and somehow she had just done something big, although I didn't know what. I put on a coat, hit the street and walked up 17th in the direction from which she had just come. I slowed down my steps. I look like a man at leisure, but not so aimless a soul as to invite the attention of the police or a mugger. I see that the rear window on the Jeep has been cracked and at the center of the spiderweb fracture is a decal proclaiming the United Gun Association. I take my new knowledge and keep walking. A minute later I am in Monk's, nodding to acquaintances and enjoying a draft glass of a very complicated Belgian ale called Kwak.

I have a tiny mystery and I am pleased with it.

12.

Paula is on her way home from work, walking through the shadows of the bare trees on the sidewalk. She's absorbed in the music of her own footsteps and the clattering of the branches in the unseasonably warm wind. A few minutes later, she comes down her stoop in a new pale gray sweat suit. She is wearing a blue reflective headband that she took some time to pick out. Around her waist is a webbed belt with a large zippered purse attached. She stops when she reaches the pavement, looks both ways and then marches vigorously off to her right, arms swinging, moving with traffic on the one-way, east-bound street. Above Paula a man sits cross-legged at one end of the dark field of roofs that make up her block. The man is sitting in the shadow of a tree trunk; all around him is the pink chemical glow of a pair of street lamps. He would be invisible from the street below. It's Cardoso.

The roof has what the real estate listings call "grt vu." For three blocks to the east there is nothing but polite little trees that frame, but do not interfere with, his view of the nighttime crowd. He can see a block north and two or three blocks south which is about as far as the fun goes.

The weather has turned cold. The warning signs of Xmas are on the street. There are knots of thoughtfully dressed people strolling, not hurrying, through the chill. Here and there are outbreaks of false jollity. A woman passes with a sprig of mistletoe, a parasitic plant with poisonous berries, pinned to her lapel. Cardoso wonders where she expects to be kissed. There is, in spite of the weather, a warm whiskyish tone to the night.

A half an hour later and half a block east on Pine, a costumed person on stilts is handing out coupons in front of a storefront bar. He is wearing a shiny blue blazer and red and white striped pants. His shirt is red flannel with tiny white buttons and his hat is soft and red with a fur band at the brow and a tuft of fur at the end of its dangling point. His beard is white and caprine, we've seen it on a recruiting poster somewhere. The buckle of his belt is just above the heads of most of the strollers and he takes extravagantly deep bows to greet them as they pass.

"Hellooo," he says, "I'm Sammy Claus and How Are Youuuu?"

His pronunciation is as mannered as his bow. The "how" has the roundest and longest vowel, the "ah" of "are" is drawn out and then abruptly yanked to heel by a gravelly growling *r* and the "you" is pushed out through obscenely pursed lips. His face, is masked with white grease paint and his lips are painted yellow green.

He greets a strolling trio: two men and a woman. The woman laughs at Sammy Claus in that demented, much obliged way that kids laugh at clowns. The men smile in hopes of moving on quickly. Two younger men in identical pea coats stop at the foot of the stilt. They raise their faces and allow that they are 'fiiine' and go on their way laughing. Paula approaches, damp and striding. Sammy cranks his bow up one extra hysteria notch for her. His arm folds into his waist and then sweeps out down and away, his fingers unfurling one by one. "How Are You?" Paula smiles, she mouths the word 'fine' and walks on, taking the smile with her.

A few minutes later, Paula climbs her stoop, her chest working visibly through the loose sweatshirt. She enters her bedroom and removes the belted purse. She throws it on the bed and it lands heavy. Paula unzips the purse, removes a pistol with a long, slender barrel and aims it at her pillow. She squeezes the trigger, flinching against the bang. There is instead a tiny whoosh of air. Paula goes to the pillow and picks up a cylindrical pellet seventeen hundredths of an inch in diameter. Propelled by the fading stored pressure of the lever-activated air gun, it has made a dent in the pillow and then rolled down to her mattress undamaged.

Cardoso's Diary 2
....

The next night, I walk past Odetta and see the red-haired waitress at work. I am home by eleven and move my club chair, the one with the sawed off rear legs, over to the front window. Trench coat and fedora at the ready. When I see her approaching, half-halting, twisting to check the rear of each car, I run down the three flights of stairs to the street, arriving just as she crosses Pine Street from the north. She sees me, she smiles, she slows, she hi howareyous. I sense that I can find out easily by interrogation disguised as conversation that which I have contrived to deduce at some pain. I decide instead that I will enjoy my seat at her unfolding in proportion to how thoroughly I keep my interest to myself. I tip my hat. I compliment her on recent lobster and tuna, smile and fix my eyes off in the middle distance. Pleasant contact, increased familiarity, nothing personal. Neither of us actually stops. Perfect. I cross the street as the light changes and she moves on. From the darkness at the far corner, I notice her climbing the stoop of 1706. Two more steps, turns back, see the outer door close behind her. I envision the fumbling at the mailbox, I scan the intersection four ways to confirm my aloneness. In less than a minute, a red cat lying across the sill of the third floor front window jumps down. A few seconds later, I see a light dimly, then another brighter one in the same window.

The next day, I stop at her house and see that the name on the 3rd floor apartment bell is Sherman. I will call the Urban Ranger.

The Ranger's real name is Harvey Lichtmann and he is a man with whom I have had a strange alliance. We are foul weather friends, faithful in the bad times, bored in the good. He holds what they call an important job at City Hall. He has held the job through the last five mayoral administrations. The newspapers credit his longevity to his superlative performance and dedication to the city. I credit it to his talent for investigation and to the certain malicious zeal with which he pursued the embarrassing details of the lives of his betters. That his dossiers included many of the newspaper and TV people in town has, no doubt, helped to insure his fame.

If the Ranger's hobby is malice, his religion is gluttony. He is not one of those soi-disant gluttons who merely overeat conspicuously for the sheer fame of it. The

Ranger is different. Food is, I once observed, the place where he held his secret rituals, said his prayers, made his vows and renegotiated them later. The Ranger's world was edible.

The Ranger and I had exchanged favors in the past. It was only a slightly unnatural liaison, like oil and egg yolk: I had worshipped rage and dabbled in gluttony. Saw his ying and raised him a yang.

The Ranger did not know about Ms. Sherman. She is not powerful enough to be worth his wiles. I left a message at his most private number. I told him the name and address and mentioned that she had served us but a few nights ago at Odetta. He returned my call within an hour; too short a time for even Harvey to conduct the most cursory public-record investigation.

"Manny, have you taken up drugs?"

"Hardly, Range."

"Been on any long vacations?"

"I would have sent you a postcard."

"Then I can't imagine how you don't know what I'm about to tell you. Your Ms Sherman was the chief witness to the murder of that poor dear boy in front of Skipper's in October. I would imagine, from her job and her friends and her unprepossessing physique that she is what is commonly and crudely called a fag-hag."

"Oh. So she saw the killing?"

"A bit more than that. The shooter held a gun to her face, pistol-whipped her, the Daily News said. She went to the ER at Graduate with facial lacerations, was being patched up when she heard that her buddy had joined the Silent Majority. Do you want anything else on her?"

"No, Range'. I think you just told me what I need to know. Thanks."

13.

The Execution is set for December 31st at 11:30 PM. Paula has a ticket to the Execution. She was entitled to one as the chief prosecution witness, she could have filed for one as a friend of the victim. She could have even filed with a good chance of success under 'neighbor' or 'interested member of the public.' The eyewitness seats are the best.

Paula could have stayed home and watched the Execution on Court TV Plus, but it's New Year's Eve and she wasn't really doing anything after work anyway. So by 10:48 she has taken her seat in the front row of the Rotunda. Paula has never attended an Execution before. She is surprised by how chilly it is inside the Rotunda and by the peculiar, non-directional quality of the light. Her seat is in the front row, very near the center.

By 10:53 she is joined by Tom's twelve-year-old sister who squeezes her hand and says "I know my Tomtom would have married you." Paula smiles at her and wraps her innocence up in her arms. The sister mistakes the gesture and hugs her back and introduces Paula to the uncle who rode in with her from Berks County and then they stop talking and settle back in the quiet whooshing expectancy of the crowd.

Most of the two hundred amphitheater seats have been taken by 11:42 when two marshals lead him in. His hands are tied in front with half-inch rope and his feet are loosely bound together with the same stuff. He shuffles. He is wearing the clothes he wore that night in front of Skipper's. Paula can see a girdle under the ski mask and a thick white fabric cord pressing his lips apart through the mouth hole. He is gagged, no further utterances.

The marshals take him to the center of the stage which is depressed slightly below the level of Paula's seat. There are two six-inch iron poles set about ten feet apart into the concrete of the stage. They are placed inside a circular rim about eight inches high that rises from the floor. Exactly between the poles there is a drain. Paula notices without interest a thick water hose on the wall to the far left of the stage. The time is kept for her and him by a digital clock on the wall behind the poles.

Paula notices that his clothes are frayed, more worn than when she last saw him at the trial. There is a smell of disinfectant and strawberries. His hands are untied from each other and immediately retied to rings set in the poles at a level slightly above his head. Paula is surprised at how much rope he is given, a maypole dancer's worth she thinks. Then his ankles are unbound and secured by five-foot lines to rings in the poles at floor level. He could click his heels or do a split.

The house lights dim and the marshals leave the stage. Two sets of floods set in the ceiling behind Paula's head gradually brighten. The man is standing, loosely attached to the poles in a two-horned cone of light. He shuffles to the left, brings his feet together and drops his left hand, almost covering his face with the gesture, then stops.

From stage left the executioner enters, a small person, dressed, as one would hope, in black, compressed, concealed and totally androgynous. He or she comes on stage carrying a sword, bouncing it lightly. The sword is about three feet long. It has a quiet, un-theatrical shine. The executioner stops almost in front of the man and points back to stage left with the sword and then delicately fastens a strap that will hold the sword's handle in place against a black leather glove. The gesture is deliberately graceful, it tells even the dullest viewer that inside the black carapace is a woman.

She turns to the man, hops onto and then down from the circular rim. She lands lightly inside the circle, facing him, knees bent, the flat of her sword resting on his hand rope, stage left. She raises the sword and runs it lightly along the rope. A pile of fibres are shaved off and fall to the ground. A soft vowel sound from the crowd. Paula is impressed by the sharpness. The chefs at work would like that. She wonders if the fibres might clog the drain.

The prisoner's eyes follow the sword and then the fall of shavings. The executioner takes a step toward the crowd and makes a stylized deep bow from the waist, the sword held wide and pointed to the floor. She straightens, steps to the side, sword still low, spins about-face, whirls the sword in an arc downupdown in a diagonal across his body. He pulls away against his ropes, the sword tip misses him and we hear in the utter stillness the ringing of the air where it was cut.

The ringing fades. Paula cannot see whether he shows surprise at his intactness. Someone in the crowd takes a breath, then another and another. Someone giggles. The executioner pauses, brings the sword backhand in an arc just above his waist. He is straining away from her, his head thrown back as the tip of the sword slices his jacket, cutting neatly through the zipper, splitting the green. There is a tiny, breathless moment, then light, scattered applause, and someone in the back yells, "Take it off, take it ALL off." The executioner knows her stagecraft: she has used up all her allowable false starts. She points her sword to the ceiling, we see a strobe flash on her blade, she draws two small circles in the air with the sword's tip, brings the sword to horizontal and zips it over his turned back face. His knees bend and his head snaps forward. Hanging from a bloody smear in the ski mask is what must be a piece of his lower lip. The gag beneath his mask is drawing some blood up into itself. Capillary action.

She turns to the audience and squats, the sword, edge up, held backwards over her shoulder like a hobo's bindlestiff. Working blind. She moves lightly, standing erect and bringing the sword up and over her shoulder towards the crowd, stepping to her right after she does. She has split his nose from underneath, only a bit to the left of center and a trickle from it is joining the main stream from his lip.

Paula has not breathed, she sees that it is 11:57. Noises outside are making their way in. She recognizes the traditional New Year's banging of pots and pans in the streets above the Rotunda. She likes that custom, so different from the sweaty indoors happy new year of the north country where she grew up.

The executioner turns back to the man and in a perfectly vertical plumb bob of a stroke slices him from the outside margin of his cheek to his shoulder and down his chest, almost to the hem of his jacket. A second vertical does the same thing on the other side. Paula is nauseated now, sees him back on the street in front of Skipper's. Death gives out onto death she figures while she wonders if the white stripes revealed by the cuts might be ribs.

She hears. She hears suggestions from the crowd. "Slash his . . . Put it in his . . . Cut off his . . ." They come mostly from the back, from people whose bad seats indicate that they did not know Tom. The front rows are silent, the noise from the back washing over them. We hear more banging of pots and the clock flips to 11:58. Paula holds Tom's sister, sometimes shielding her eyes, sometimes hiding behind her like she used to hide behind Tom. The banging gets louder, sword cuts ring, meat cuts sing. Paula lets out her breath, takes a bite of air and chews it up. We hear singing and another swing of the sword. She recognizes the melody.

She is on her feet, pulling the girl with her and the breath shoots from her chest, catching the lyric

. . . lang syne, my dear

For auld lang syne

We'll drink a cup of kindness yet

For the sake of auld lang syne

The audience is rising in ones and threes, singing along, incontinently repeating the few lyrics they know over and over again, but Paula is back in college chorus, each verse coming out with a pure clear burst that sweeps up a few stragglers and carries the song along, they the rumbling accompaniment for Paula whose arms pull the girl tighter in to her chest and whose voice rises to the ceiling up and falling up higher and higher. Still.

Cardoso's Diary 3

I am moved: a little by my knowledge of this peculiar secret and a lot more by the power of the girl. I've been wounded myself. I suspect that if she is emptied, her emptiness is charged like a Leyden Jar with cracking energy. I feel, through her, some of life's pleasant edgy unbalance returning to me.

I call a friend. Her name is Connie Battaglia and she shares with her cousin of the same name a small catering operation in South Philadelphia. Connie is lean and spare, long black hair on skinny shoulders, grace in her spidery arms. I am shaken by her beauty and disabled by recent events from acting on the shakes. She is the most utterly candid person I've ever known. No candles to the saints of tact or dissimulation are on fire at her house.

Her splendid candor no doubt accounts for her lack of suitors. Connie is as frightening as Truth and her strange scrawny beauty does not countervail in her world. Undervalued asset.

A few months ago, I had my hands on her bare skin and I heard her yesyesyes and turned away. Later, on the night that my world turned around again, she sent me a note. It said: Hey, Killer, give me a call will ya?

I call.

"Connie, it's Manny"

"I could tell. How the hell are ya?"

"God, I don't know but I miss you. I'd like to see you"

"Well, I'm gonna be in your neighborhood tomorrow night."

"Can we have dinner?"

"I tell ya, I'm going to a book signing at Borders. Why doncha come with me and we'll figure out something from there."

The signing at Borders was for a book called "Biting the Apple: Loving Men More, Needing Men Less." It seemed that every middle-class woman in the city had to have this book and most of them had to be there to get their copy signed. The store gave them all apples as they walked in the door, crisp just-harvested winesaps that snapped to the teeth. Connie and I found ourselves in a sea of attractive women of all ages: snapping apple biters, munching and exchanging thoughts about the philosophy of love and romance.

We love the soundtrack and the sharp smell of fruit, giggle at the spectacle. We get our apples, talk about love in the modern world. I see Connie reflected in a window, watch her turn from full face to profile, want to touch that face.

I buy a copy, Connie buys two. When the green-eyed beauty who wrote the book signs them, she smiles at us mistaking us perhaps, for lovers. I see that the author has a flake of apple skin between her teeth and I swear to myself that I will always be her fan.

"Ya know what's wrong with my romantic philosophy Manny? I'm more of a man than any of the men I know."

"Try saying that with a Granny Smith in your mouth."

We have dinner at Origlio's and over veal chops and white beans, I tell her the story of Ms. Sherman, the pistol packin' waitron. I'm surprised that I'm telling her and suddenly aware that I don't want secrets. I ask her to keep this story to herself.

She says "Do you want to fuck her?"

"Well, no . . . but there's something about watching her that makes me want to make love again." In fact, I may be lying.

"You don't seem like the kinda guy who'd get hot for weapons. I always figured you'd be a pushover for a woman with a nice hot brasciole and bottle of Brunello."

I try to explain and she stops me. She says that my guilty secret is safe with her. Besides, she has a cousin who does auto glass and it's got to be good for his business. We talk about food and wine, gossip about some friends. She touches my hand a lot. For emphasis.

Later, as the cab is about to swallow her up, she asks me if I know the difference between pussy and parsley. I don't. "Manny, Manny," she says, "nobody eats parsley," and she leaves me on the sidewalk, blinking at the dark.

The light is low and from the east. Paula is jogging on Pine Street, going with the traffic. She passes the florist's shop where the Valentine's Day Special is a Dozen Long-Stemmed Roses—$24.95. Something on the curbside catches her eye and she slows down, runs in place, scans the street. Seeing another pedestrian, she resumes her run, making a right turn at the next corner. We watch the same spot and in a minute or so, Paula returns running in the same direction. Paula has made four right turns and come around the block, full circle. Once again she turns in the same spot, this time seeing no one. She unzips her purse and draws the air pistol, aims and fires. She pulls a lever on the side of the gun and returns it to her purse, zips and runs off. The action has taken just over four seconds. She yearns for replay, aches for slo-mo.

Instead she begins to sing to herself in a mock baritone. It is Verdi: The Anvil Chorus.

Chi del gitano i giorni abella? La zingarella!

Who makes the gypsy's days beautiful? The gypsy girl!

With each measure she imagines a vignette, windshield, UGA decal, pistol, crack, shatter. Some shatter in the dark, some in the light. After a dozen or so, her brain has conjured all the decals it can and she imagines waves of illuminated safety glass fragments that are thrown up from one side or another. As she comes to the end of the chorus, she hears the blending of a thousand points of tinkling lighted glass. It reminds her of the waves on the rocks and a summer day in Maine years ago when she was young.

15. ✸

The newscaster is bosomy and beautiful, lush and vaguely southern. In contravention of the universal custom with newscasters, she seems to know the meaning of the words she reads. She smiles at odd moments, looks at the lens with arched eyebrow.

"Here's some shattering news. They're calling it the St. Valentine's Day Massacre, but it wasn't marked by minced Chicago mobster. This kinder, gentler slaying was confined to car windshields in several Center City Neighborhoods. According to Police spokesman Det. Alan Sloane, some time between 9 PM on Valentine's Day and 6 AM today, a gang of people went on a rampage, shooting out the rear windows of parked cars. Police estimate that over forty car windows were shattered in that time period. Most of the car owners reported that nothing was taken."

Paula hears this last sentence sitting cross-legged on her bed. The old TV has been replaced by a newer color set and as the story ends, Paula dismisses the newslady with a flick-wrist poke of the remote control. Paula is smiling, bouncing on the bed and hugging her knees.

A slow panning, PBS-style montage of headlines. They are not in 96-point, WAR OVER type, but the more modestly scaled first-page-of-the-features-section-below-the-fold font.

St. Louis Post Dispatch
PHILLY GETS KICKED IN THE GLASS

Chicago Tribune
VALENTINE'S DAY GLASSACRE

Los Angeles Times
WINDSHIELD WIPEOUT

Manny Cardoso is leaning, facing right against a double-hung sash window. He has a telephone pinched between his shoulder and ear and he is reading aloud from a tabloid newspaper.

"According to police sources, all of the vandalized windshields bore United Gun Association stickers of one sort or another. The investigation of the incidents is proceeding on the assumption that this was a co-ordinated attack launched simultaneously by several people in different locations throughout the city."

The person he's reading to is a woman in chef whites seated at a desk in a cramped office. On her desk are the ruins of lunch and some untidy paper towers. She has pale skin, hazel eyes and a mop of black hair barely restrained in a loose ponytail. Through the glass behind her a teenage boy is working an automatic slicing machine. The woman is moving in a slow wriggly seated dance as she listens. She is holding the phone with two hands. One hand is pressing it to her ear and the other is lightly stroking it. The gesture should be ludicrous and it's not.

Cardoso continues. "In an apparently unrelated incident, a car bearing a similar decal was vandalized by having a brick thrown through its windshield. Two teenaged boys, one wearing a Friends Academy jacket, were spotted running away from the scene, but no arrests were made." The woman's smile develops a little twist.

"I really like the idea of two spotted teenaged boys. It kinda turns me on. Does it say what color the spots are and where you can pick up a pair of spotted boys for one's own self?"

"You have a filthy mind, Connie."

"Thank you. So do you think your little waitress has a gang?"

"Could be, or maybe she took a lot of cabs."

"Well, she sounds like quite a woman." She stops moving, stroking: the smile disappears but her voice is unchanged. "Do you have any plans for her now?"

"I have to admit she's inspired me and yeah, as a matter of fact, I do have plans, but they don't have anything to do with her." He sets the paper down and both of his hands go to the phone. "I was wondering. . ."

Paula is walking vigorously west on Pine Street between tussocks of dirty white snow. She's singing the English madrigal "Lately Came I Unto You." She has new jogging clothes. The sweat suit has been replaced by a pair of spandex full-length tights, pale blue. She sings:

Lately came I unto you
A pale depression on my soul,
But soon I left abiding too
The broken pieces all made whole.

Paula is proud. She feels the pride as a lump in her chest below the collarbone. The feeling isn't about her voice, it's about her legs. The jogging in pursuit of decals has not been in vain. The muscles are contoured and firm: sinuous ropes not random parsnipy lumps. She watches their reflections in shop windows and in the eyes of men on the street. The voice she's had all her life, she's never had legs before. Paula is running now, running away from us. Running through the streets while the streets have been running through her. Her ass is no longer just the sinker that keeps her bait on the bottom. It is a working asset. As she accelerates eastward on Pine Street, she puffs out the last verse of the madrigal:

So well I learned the Doctor's Art
Under your sweet tuition,
That now you've gone and though I mourn, ·
I 'm become my own physician.

Paula's watching TV again. The picture shrinks with a simulated voltage drop and then swells again. It may be swelling in response to the Newslady. For the evening news she is wearing an evening gown, her desk has been replaced with a cocktail table. She is sitting beside not behind and the only thing on the table is a tall flute-like glass with a straw colored effervescent liquid in it.

Newslady's dress is floor length with a very deeply cut décolletage and paved with the little glass cylinders that are called bugle beads. It is held up at the shoulders by broad straps that end in outjagging epaulets.

The beads catch the light and throw it back in flashes to the lens. The flashes offset but do not distract from the sweep of the exposed Newslady bosom. The U of the neckline dives to a few inches above her navel. It is wide enough to imagine that the tiniest gesticulation will present us with the Newslady Nipple.

She smiles, lowers her chin and tilts her head slightly, forehead to the right. Her better angle. She welcomes the viewers to the Evening News and raises her tableside hand, reaching out and exposing an ivory muscled inner arm. We switch to the camera with the long view and see what the hand was waiting for. A young white man comes on stage. He is wearing a winged cap and winged slippers and a tiny creamy loin cloth. He has been zoned Lean/Muscular, Overbuilding Not Permitted.

He walks with deliberate haste to the Newslady's table and hands her a sheet of paper. Newslady smiles up at him, her smile aiming for a spot in the middle of his chest. She glances at the paper, sets it on the table and turns back to us. The dress has shifted only slightly, enough to assure us that we are looking at separate, permutable layers. She is a creature, not a casting. She reads: "Who says it's a toll-free road? At approximately 12:15 this morning, Josef Repax of the Fairmount Section was driving south on the expressway when his rear window suddenly shattered. There was only one other car on the road behind him and it immediately swung onto an off-ramp. Repax called police on his wireless phone, but no arrests were made."

Another youth with a Euro-chic scowl and the same costume as the first strides out from the other side of the stage. Paper, smile, glance.

"In another auto-glass incident, three truck windows were smashed in the parking lot of Jezebel's, a gentleman's club on Delaware Avenue. The vandalism occurred sometime after midnight as crowds were leaving the Frank Zappa Memorial Concert at the nearby Spectrum VII auditorium."

The Newslady's frisson suggests that she may know more than she's letting on. It does not, alas, jiggle her loose from her beaded breastplate and the screen goes dark.

16.

Dawn. Philadelphia's streets were laid out in a grid in 1674. The grid is tilted a few degrees counter clockwise of north. Its perfect squareness helped traffic to flow and enabled visitors to find their way around the city that was to become the first capital of the United States. It also allows, for a few months a year, the dramatic low-angle light in which Paula is returning from her morning run.

She is heading east along Pine, into the light, her breath making little cottony clouds that are blown away by the wind of her steady six miles an hour. Her weird puffy earmuffs with a chinstrap make her head look like a portable radio.

She is slowing as much as she dares, wanting to cool down but not freeze. She jogs in place to let a truck pass as another athlete shuffles to the same corner from the other side of the angle. He is in his thirties, pale and rounded, a soft-edged man a bare inch taller than Paula. He wears an orange sweatshirt that says HOBART in purple block letters. His baggy cotton pants are faded gray and he is wearing a pair of loose navy blue shorts over them, covering their nakedness. His glasses are held on with an elastic band that cinches a head of curly blue-black hair. He slows his pace to speak to her.

Paula recognizes him. She's seen him around the neighborhood, all pinstripes and Burberry, on his way home from work as she's been going in. Small double take, the new context lets her smile. She whips the earmuffs off, tucks them beneath her arms.

Her ears begin to sting. She welcomes the feeling, is secretly glad to be feeling anything at all. He stops, feet moving in grape-pressing cadence.

She knows that what she says doesn't matter. All that counts is the body language: tilt the head, drop the arms, keep smiling. He smiles, nods, she smiles, laughs. Even with a sweatsuit padding her, she now has a waist, a little tuck-in between the upper and the lower. Paula reaches down to her purse. She reaches inside. Is she going to shoot him? Is there a UGA decal on his glasses?

No no, it's the familiar-face-gets-a-name moment. Very tender, very dear. She's not afraid of him. Couldn't be. Daniel, he says his name is, Daniel Farber. There's more. She's seen him around the neighborhood. It's hard to be afraid of somebody when you've seen him buy prune juice in the supermarket or watched him carry a ball of dirty shirts under his arm.

There is a gentleness to his face, a grace that perches somewhere around his eyes. He makes a small, self-diminishing joke, she laughs. She doesn't feel much like a date, but then he doesn't look much like one either. Daniel, she has decided, is too soft and accepting, the kind of man who plays easy-to-get: Not Her Type.

To the tune of their slowly decreasing heart beats, Paula unzips her purse. Will she shoot him anyway? God, this is a tough neighborhood. No, she pulls out a small pad and a stub pencil. The pad has a collection of license plate numbers and street addresses, and she quickly flips to a new page. She writes her phone number, tears off the sheet and hands it to him.

When she gets home, Paula finds a tape: Mom and Dad—Carousel. She presses PLAY and hears her parents singing "When the Children Are Asleep." Dad's voice is strong and precise, a near-baritone and her mother's alto weaves around it. Paula notices for the first time the erotic coloring of their voices together. She is embarrassed by it a little bit, the more so because the tinkly piano playing in the background is her own.

The Hairy Mary Show

"Good afternoon everybody, it's time to kick off your hat, hang up your shoes, tell the boss to take a hike and settle in with the Hairy Mary Show. I'm Hairy Mary Shefady and I'm here to bring you an hour of the weirdest stuff on earth, every bit of it straight from local newspapers around the country and around the world. Just remember, if we want real weirdness, we don't need space aliens, we don't need Bigfoot, one, two, three (sings), We got each other.

"And now to today's stories. From Philadelphia comes news of a gang of vandals taking aim at the super-macho Yoo Gee Ay! In Topeka, Kansas, a man burglarizing a closed convenience store is caught when he locks himself in and calls police for assistance. And get this one, a study by the American Association for Quality Education (also known as QUANE) discovers that up to 22% of college teachers may not be able to read and write!

"Our number one story today comes from Philadelphia. Over Valentine's Day weekend, a gang of sharpshooters fanned out over the City of Brotherly Shove and shot out the windows of eighty-seven cars and trucks. That's strange enough to win the Hairy Mary Furball of the Day Award all by itself, but wait, as they say on late night TV, there's more. Every single blown out windshield had a decal or sticker supporting the United Gun Association. Boom! Whaddya think of that one?

"Let's go to the phones, weird ones! I've got Patrish calling from Dallas. Hey what's weird Patrish?"

Patrish: (laughing) "More than you know, Mary. Hey, I used to live in Philadelphia and I can't imagine that a gang could run around the streets shooting off guns and not attract some attention. I mean that's eighty-seven loud bangs in a place with a lot of neighborhoods. Didn't anybody call the cops? If they didn't, that could be the weirdest part of the whole thing."

Hairy Mary: "Good question. Wait a minute . . . yeah . . . it says here that inside some of the cars they found pellets like the ones they use in air rifles. So instead of a Big Bang it was just a frosty fart. I guess nobody heard."

Patrish: "You mean they did it with BB guns? C'mon Mary, you trying to tell us that there's a militia armed with BB guns that's sworn to attack the UGA?"

Hairy Mary: "You're right. That is strange. Do they line up at the Liberty Bell, you suppose? These militia guys always dress funny, like they wanna be guards at the Nixon White House. All right, Hairy Mary offers a *five hundred dollar reward to the person who sends me a genuine photograph of the BB Militia. Thanks for calling Patrish, I've got Larry from Arlington, Virginia. Hiya Larry."*

Larry: "Hello Mary. I just wanted to tell you that the same thing happened in a crowded parking lot outside The Elks' hall here last weekend. Except instead of BBs, they found great big steel ball bearings, like something that might be fired from a slingshot."

Hairy Mary: "Well folks down in Virginia must have just discovered what every politician in America knows."

Larry: "What's that, Mary?"

Hairy Mary: "That it takes steel balls to go up against the UGA! (makes rude noise) Thanks for calling Larry, stay weird. I got another Larry, this one's from Leucadia, California. Am I worried about the 'Curse of the Two Larrys?' Uh uh. Welcome whacko, what's up?"

Leucadia Larry: "Hi Mary, I just want to say "way to crime Philly!" I mean kids out here are spray painting their names on palm trees and using skateboards to scare pedestrians. You guys back there are doing something great. Keep it up."

Hairy Mary: "So Larry, If we find the BB militia, should we give 'em your name? You wanna join up?"

Larry: "Well, maybe, I don't know if I . . ."

Hairy Mary: "What's a matter, Larry, don't you like funny hats? Or maybe, wait, this could be it, maybe you don't have steel balls (Loud rude noise). Thanks for calling, Larry. Each of today's callers gets a tube of Hairy Mary Mustache Wax and our hairfelt thanks. If you think you're weird enough, give us a call. "Now let me tell you about my candidate for the title of the world's dumbest burglar. . ."

17.

Paula's bedroom, Paula in the tight blue running pants, mega-super running shoes, and one of those new All-You semi-transparent sports bras. Her hand is reaching for a brown over-the-shoulder bag. She reaches into it and feels the pistol. Its muzzle is resting in a funnel that Paula has cut in an end seam. The barrel is held in place by the same lacing that holds the closure for the bag. She has cut a slit in the side of the bag just in front of the trigger.

Paula's fingers pry at a lever that unfolds itself from alongside the barrel. Twisting the gun slightly, she pulls the lever away from the barrel and lets it fall back. Cocked. She puts her head through the bag's strap so that the strap is over her left shoulder and the bag hangs at her right side. She straightens her spine, rolls her pelvis back, checks the mirror, smiles. 'Posture' as her Aunt Mimi used to say she says now to herself.

She zippers the bag. Her hand pinions the purse to her side as she turns on her heel. Her fingers find the slit, then the trigger, a whoosh of air and Paula looks across the room to where she has assembled twenty thicknesses of corrugated board. At least two trips to the liquor store, two clumsy portages of empty whisky boxes. The stack is propped on a folding chair and there is a pink sheet of paper taped to it.

Paula crosses the room in three steps. Her fingers lift the paper on its cellophane hinge. The pellet has pierced the paper about three inches low and to the left of a thick X mark in the paper's center. Paula flips an eyebrow up, drops a mouth corner down. She is not pleased, not displeased either.

Paula's a musician, she knows how to practice, she understands concentration and the power of repetition. She spins, hears the whooshes, watches the march of the pellet holes toward the X.

Later, in her black trench coat, she puts on the shoulder bag, pulls the lever, adjusts the rough knit scarf so that the fringe hangs just below the trigger finger slit in the outside of the purse. She checks herself in the mirror over the dresser, straightens her spine. The top of the dresser is clean. Tidied. Paula gives herself a little nod, almost a wink. The door to her apartment closes, the locks twistywristed closed. A few seconds later Paula goes down the steps and out into the city. Cocked.

18.

The man with Paula's phone number is Daniel Farber, thirty years old, Penn Law School grad. Primary Occupation; intellectual property law for Children's Television Workshop. He also volunteers in the Office of the Children's Advocate in City Hall.

His hair is curly black and dense, cut just short enough for office work. His nose is large and sharp, his eyes are big and his chin is tucked under and back from his full lips. He is freshly shaven. The effect is of an alert, sensuous animal, a fox, an otter, a dolphin gone to land.

Daniel is sitting at an oak roll-top desk, working at a one-piece, mahogany-toned Apple Ten. He is typing passionately, squinting occasionally and biting his lip. The desk is against a wall and on the wall above the desk there is a pink plastic hippopotamus lamp that is glowing faintly.

On the very top of the desk and to the right of the lamp there is a painted statue of a woman warrior of Homer's time. Two matte board museum signs are posted on the wall. They abut each other and are halfway between the two artifacts. The sign on the left says Hippo Light, the one on the right says Hippolyte.

His face is working, squinting, lip biting, eyebrow dipping, nostril pinching. He seems to care about what he's writing. Beyond Daniel there is a window filled with afternoon light. Outside it there's a brownstone row house, crisper, cleaner, more authoritative than Paula's. The stoop is marble, the doorknob is brass, strips of lead crisscross the window in the first floor apartment.

A few minutes later, Daniel opens the door to the street. He's wearing his orange and gray jogging clothes and dropping his way down the stoop to the sidewalk. He checks his watch and turns left in a slow but determined walk. The street is better tended and less traveled than Pine; doors are grander, street trees corralled in wrought iron.

He passes a figure in white slowly sweeping invisible trash to the curb. At the first corner, he stops and looks in all four directions. He is looking for Paula, hoping to see her again, ask her to dinner and avoid the dreaded "Hi, I'm Daniel" phone call, the one where he has to hope she remembers who he is and where he may have to stutter his way through reminding her. The thought of that phone call puts his heartbeat up in the training zone. He doesn't see her, even though he doubles his usual stretching routine and so he begins a slow shuffle north, toward Rittenhouse Square and the heart of the city.

19.

From the crowded back seat of a car, Paula picks out the enamel road sign in the headlights. It says Colmar, and the arrow points to the right. The road leads through industrial suburban sprawl, down a little hill, left at the gas station, second building on the right. Romantic notions being crushed on every side. Paula and four other servers climb out behind a one-and-a-half-story cinder block building with two twenty-foot roll-up garage doors let in to about sixty feet of front. The sign above the doors, in red plastic letters on white, says

COLMAR VOLUNTEER FIRE COMPANY, Eng. #2

Colmar. Oh yes, Colmar, Pennsylvania. There is music coming from a second squat building behind the first and Paula makes her way there. This Colmar is American. Paula enters the hall through the kitchen entrance, passes the dishwasher and its hum and for a second the clatter of plates drowns out the music.

It's a Sunday night wedding, restaurant closed, and she's picking up a few bucks working for the caterer. By ten o'clock, dinner is over. She has an oval brown plastic tray on her shoulder. The tray is loaded with used coffee cups and lily-like glass ice cream dishes. Paula waits behind another server and then spins her tray down and slides it through a slot onto a stainless steel counter

She taps a woman on the shoulder and with two fingers pulls an invisible cigarette to and from her lips. The woman, older than Paula, face all frown lines and lipstick, nods, and Paula snakes her way through fellow workers. She leaves the kitchen by the door near the dishwasher and steps out into the night. There is a faint, familiar pink light in the parking lot and Paula sees cotton candy breath. She flicks the collar of her trench coat up and slips on a pair of black gloves. She has her purse.

Moving quickly, she follows the archipelago of shadows to the other side of the parked cars. They are mostly turned toward the fire hall and so she is facing their rear ends. Bruce Springsteen is singing "Glory Days" and we hear a hoot and then laughter.

She moves quickly from the shadows to the farthest line of cars. Time to inspect the troops, shoot the losers. She doesn't notice that not all the cars are empty. She sets her purse on the trunk of a big gray sedan and fingers the warm waiting slit. The UGA decal proclaims its owner LIFE MEMBER. Paula loves the irony, (got much life in your member, buster?) she aims for the muscular arm brandishing a rifle in a circle of gold. Whoosh of air, the small sharp crack and she fancies that she sees the pellet, dancing in celebration, rise up into the air and toward the light.

She swings the purse away from the car, re-cocks the pistol and moves on. Beside a small pickup with a rifle rack in the back, she kneels to adjust her angle, placing the ricochet like a good bank shot. She squeezes. Whoosh crack.

Paula turns as she rises and steps into the aisle. She turns right quickly. As she approaches the next car, the passenger door opens. She freezes and the driver's door opens a second later. In the back light, she can see that they are men, one tall, one not. The shorter one is wearing, incredibly, a cowboy hat.

They exchange looks, close the car doors with exaggerated slowness and walk toward her. Their feet make liquid sounds in the stones of the parking lot. "Ma'am" the tall one says, his right hand holding something close to his body at the hip. Paula takes another step. Standing by the trunk of the car, they will sandwich her on either side in another second. What did they see? Can she run? Where would she hide? The light is full in her face, they would recognize her easily.

Some vague central place that she thinks of as her insides is alive, on fire. Seconds break into fragments, pennies from the dollar, and as each one goes by she examines it. The shorter man clears his throat and reaches inside his jacket. Paula expects the badge, the cuffs.

He brings out a pack of cigarettes and at the same instant she smells the marijuana smoke that puffed out of the car doors and clings to them.

"Evening, Ma'am" he says, and she can see, as he walks away from her, that his mouth is pulled back in a silly grin. The tall man waves his beer bottle at her as he passes. The night has never been so beautiful or the music half as good.

And all we were talkin' about
was Glory Days.

Cardoso's Diary 4
....

I have become, in a gentle and uncompelled sort of way, an observer of my aveng-
ing waitress. I know now, from paying attention at Odetta's, that her first name is
Paula. She told me one night as she laid down a plate of venison carpaccio, that she
has seen me stoop-sitting with my cat. I introduce myself and mention that I have
seen her out running and her face reddens and she looks down and away, telling me
that she particularly enjoys her afternoon runs.

I do not tell her that I know about her project. I do not want to scare her. I don't tell
her that I am rolling her audacity around on my tongue and savoring its richness while
I admire the way it draws on the flavor of the east coast earth. I don't tell her that I am
feeding on it, root hairs sucking up the nitrogen of her rampage.

I don't mention that I've seen her from the rooftop, I don't tell her how much I thrill
to her gall. I don't tell her that I notice, that I've counted, that it is divided into three
parts: afternoon expeditions on which I assume she writes down license plates and
locations, and morning, then evening runs on which she does her smashing.

She brings me a plate of Yellow Eye soup—little drops of curry oil winking up
from the surface of a puree of white beans—and asks me if I run myself. I don't tell
her that I have no idea who runs my self, I tell her that I row.

There is a squab, blood red meaty, hacked and stacked, pieces in a pile. The pile
rests on a foundation of glace de viande, the rich meat extract that, along with the
pyramid arrangement, is a signature of Odetta's food. I ask her how she likes it here
and I see it was the wrong question. I want to tell her that I know, that I know about
the boy and gun in her face and that I know how scarce love is and how easily it
breaks.

I backpedal, I compliment the glace. She tells me what I already know; that it is
brought in from another restaurant, a place called Fran's on the Main Line, that Fran
named this, his second restaurant, after a folk singer whose record he wore out when
he was ten. She tells me that Fran keeps this small place in town to try out new food
and to give his younger cooks a place to play.

I continue my researches. I have moved my reading chair, swinging it toward the window that faces Pine Street. I blocked up the two sawn-off rear legs so that I have an easy view of the street.

Several days ago, on a crazy cold late afternoon, I saw her walking with a stocky young man in running clothes. She was cooling down, he had not yet warmed up. I liked him, my amicability hormones provoked because his sweatshirt advertised HOBART, a brand of kitchen equipment. Hobart made the giant mixer in which I used to conjure twenty-four quarts of flour into daily bread. I felt connected, I wished them couplehood and a warm, draft-free place to rise.

Perhaps coincidentally, at about that time an itchy horny leavening began intruding itself into my blankness. I found myself wishing for the company of friends. I found myself dreaming of Connie.

20.

Harvey Lichtmann, the Urban Ranger, is standing on a low stool next to an aquarium. He is holding a small cylindrical container, the kind that usually carries a single serving of wonton soup. He is picking meal worms from it, and tossing them gently on the surface of the water. He has placed one carefully between two large goldfish and he is anticipating the race for the protein when the phone rings.

"Lichtmann here."

"Hello Range. It's Cardoso. I was wondering if you'd been following the story of the broken windshields?"

"You mean the BB Bandits story? Of course, of course. You know they struck again on Sunday? Yes, I was getting a loaf of bread at Metropolitan when I saw this monstrously tacky couple standing on the sidewalk, shaking their heads over the broken side window of their station wagon. A shard of glass with the polychrome UGA emblem was still attached to the rubber gasket that had embraced it in life. I assumed from their wildly inappropriate outfits that they had been in attendance at the Church of Everybody's Wrong But Me on the corner of Seventeenth and Spruce."

"Did you offer consolation?"

"Definitely. I strode over with my loaf of *pane stirato* under one arm and inquired politely if anything had been taken."

"Had it?"

"He thought not, although they were reluctant to enter the car just then, the presence of the devil inside no doubt. It was fun actually, watching this fellow trying to be indignant, manly and Christian all at once. He was wearing a short windbreaker over a cheap suit. The waistband on the jacket made the suit jacket stick out so he looked like he was sporting a gabardine tutu. And then he started twitching. Meanwhile his wife, who was wearing one of those virostop masks, was looking at the hole where the window had been and looking at the pile of glass and you could see the money look in her eyes. The mask, of course, rendered her mute. I actually felt a bit sorry for her."

"You did?"

"Yes, but of course when I reflected that if the fellow can pay his UGA dues and then run down to the shooting range and blast away money that could be better spent on fine old claret . . . well, I felt much better about the whole thing. In fact, I walked off humming the witch's theme from Swan Lake."

"Sounds like this gang of pellet heads made your day."

"Indeed, if I met them in a bar and they identified themselves, I would stand a round of drinks."

"Well, Ranger," Cardoso's voice cracks a bit, "do you have any idea of who these people are?"

"No, but whoever they are, God bless them."

"Yeah. Me too . . . um Range', I'd be curious to know who they are. If you run across anything, even if you hear anybody talking about it, let me know."

"Well, I'm sort of busy right now, but if anything comes my way, I will let you know."

"I tell you what . . . if you come up with something good, there's a trip to my secret fugu spot in it for you."

The Urban Ranger pokes the phone to silence, and sets it down on a small table beside a plate with a pair of chopsticks. Fugu, of course, is the blowfish that sometimes contains a deadly toxin. In a whirl of wonder about food and death, and the value of information these days; in a perfect puzzle about who eats whom, he smiles and smacks his lips.

C a r d o s o ' s   D i a r y   5

My call to the Ranger was strictly prophylactic. Paula was attracting attention, she was making the UGA look stupid, too many people were enjoying their discomfiture in public. Worse yet, she could end up making the police look stupid. I knew that an alerted Ranger would hear if the police set up a task force and I would have a chance to warn Paula.

I was enchanted by Paula's spree. I loved watching her body tighten and her spirit loosen. More than that, I seemed to be returning to life by being near, by watching her from my window and my rooftop. It was magic. So there was a danger in mentioning the case to the Ranger. It was possible that he would find this mystery of some personal interest and decide to solve it himself. If he showed signs of that, I would be forced to either warn Paula that he was on to her or beg him to lay off. In either case, the spell would be broken and I would no longer be watered by her storm. I wasn't scared, but I could imagine the dryness and the thirst.

In the meantime, I had a date to cook for. Connie, shining spider lady, truth-telling Connie was coming to dinner. This morning I woke up before the cat and in a flash, saw the entire meal in my mouth's eye. For the appetizer, I would get two huge sea scallops and slice them into five thin circular slices. I'd overlap the slices in a five-pointed star on small sheets of parchment paper and brush a little bit of saffron oil on them. Then I'd flip the sheets scallop side down into a medium-hot skillet and cook them for a minute or less, enough to edge the gold of the oil with brown. The heat would release enough moisture to free the scallops from the paper, so I'd pick up the little pentagons very carefully and transfer them to plates. Then quickly, a lemon beurre blanc sauce made with lobster butter gets dribbled over the top of the scallops in a zigzag and a few dots of red caviar. No—make that dots of red and black caviar, an egg at a time. I'll be ol' mama sturgeon swimming along sprinkling little life loads on the water.

Main course. I'll get two duck breasts and rub cracked black pepper onto them. Then wrap 'em tight and let them sit in the cold and think about themselves for a while. I'll reduce some Port in a skillet and add concentrated veal stock, three ice cubes worth from the freezer. Okay, preheat the oven, pop the breasts into skillet number two, roll 'em around, get 'em brown, then dump the reduction in the pan and put the whole thing in the oven.

Asparagus just came in the market, early stuff, but pretty. Eight spears of asparagus, erect and waiting, de-spiked but not skinned, into a wire basket, into a pot of simmering water. Two minutes, out, drain. Pull the duck breasts, cut off the tapered ends, save 'em for breakfast. Slice the rest of the breast into maybe six rounds, lay them in an overlapping line on the circumference of the plate. Spoon the reduction sauce over them. Arrange the asparagus so that each spear points to a slice of meat and all the stems come together. No. Wait. The plate is bare. Got to keep it simple, can't let it seem sparse. Got it. Strips of Orange rind, tiny threads, make them in a second with a zesting tool, sprinkle them around. Goes with the meat, goes with the veg. Confetti, festive and ain't we festing?

Dessert, wait, no. Connie doesn't eat dessert. Damn, main seduction course, woman doesn't like it. No Legs In The Air Mousse Au Chocolat, no Phallic Fingers with Homemade Mascarpone and Coffee Syrup.

"What is that cheese? yumm umm."

"It's called Mascarpone, I made it especially for you."

"You made it? Made it! Mmm, I didn't know you could do that."

And somehow, I've found, one passionate mouth-filled enthusiasm sometimes leads to another and goddamn, the woman doesn't eat dessert. I'll do something that's not quite. Slices of mango with lemon juice and cayenne or—

Sauternes. That's it, sauternes. There's something in the wine room. I know it, yes, half-bottle. Reiussec maybe or—yes, there. Chateau d'Yquem, 1982, three hundred and seventy fuckin' five sweet-assed milliliters of concentrated passion. Noble rot your moral fiber. Rock you to your bones wine, synaesthesia wine, make you see things, take you places wine. I'll put that bottle in the refrigerator now.

21.

Daniel is trailing an odor of ominous cleanliness; institutional soap and shampoo. Then it fades, refined in its passing by a tingle of vanilla, musk and bay rum. Paula did remember him and they are going out tonight and he has cashed in one anxiety for another.

Daniel's in his undershirt, fighting off first-date nausea. His fingers are paging through a line of plaid shirts hanging in a bleached wood armoire. The color of Paula's hair flashes in front of his eyes. Daniel's own hair is sculpted in place, curls at attention, a razor pinkness to his neck, new haircut. His movements are oddly formal, gestures squared off at the corners.

Three shirts to the right of his point of origin, Daniel's fingers do an about face, march two shirts to the left and stop. It's a blue plaid number, muted, rich. Daniel slips his arm in the sleeve, light starch, as he worries about what to do on his date with this brand new, neighborly woman.

He thinks about Geek Chorus, the cyber-erotic audience participation drag show that aerosols syntho-sex pheromones into the theater. He could show off, score a pair of house seats from the stage manager who used to work with him at Children's Television Workshop. But that would be excessive, and besides, in Daniel's mind, Geek Chorus was more of a third or fourth date kind of thing.

They could do what he usually did on first dates: stroll the gay zone. The idea had its points. A dozen clubs, another twenty bars and cafés. Street shows, boutiques. Its own police force. Safe but over-priced. He would seem to be trying too hard for someone he met so casually. He needs something effortless, no matter how hard it is.

An hour and a half later, Daniel and Paula are facing a man whose face is painted gold except for a circle of green around his mouth. The face is thick and reassuring, otherwise anonymous beneath the paint. The face's own daughter would not look at him and squeal "There's

Daddy." He looks directly at Daniel and Paula, smiles, leans back, comes forward, sticks a bright red tongue at them, wiggles it from side to side and settles his face into an idiot grin. His face is framed in a gold band that radiates white ostrich feathers. He is wearing a military jacket, green sequined. Its yellow epaulettes are moving, lurching, many legged, one end anchored, the other reaching to heaven in tiny insect spasms, clicking tiny black jaws in a rhythm that matches the sound as it comes up. Paula almost recognizes him, doesn't, stops trying.

They hear the banjos, a million or so. The gold-faced man is one of a corps of eight or nine, their millions an amplified effect. They are arrayed in a loose diamond in the center of what might have once been a playground. The chain-link fence is hung with loose sheets of Recyc™ bullet-proof drapery. The drapes have been painted artlessly to suggest the exotic. Palm trees, pirates dancing with monkeys, bedouins with swords chasing grass-skirted hula girls through a green and violet jungle.

It's Mummerland™, an Urban Village™ Theme Park.

The banjo players are making their way slowly through a crowd with a short, side shuffle step. Keeps you moving, don't take you nowhere. In Philadelphia, that little dance is called a Mummers' Strut, although there doesn't seem to be much strutting to it. The crowd parts for them. Slick depilated heads of young people, hair and scalp landscaped into topiary mazes, bounce and flash as they pass.

Behind the banjo corps, a dozen customers of the Mummerland Fun Park are following along, imitating the shuffle step. Some of them are holding their arms wing-like out to their sides and pivoting with each step. A few, recognizable from their jackets as the Famous Shuffling Dervishes of South Philadelphia, have their eyes closed. The tune is called "Golden Slippers," one of a handful of classics of the genre.

There is a woman who throws her head in a down circle with each side step, spinning a pony tail of dark brown hair around a jellied and polished scalp. In a pause between swings you can see a row of studs implanted above each eyebrow. The studs have little diamonds backed with light emitting diodes and the refractions of their light seem to blink like a pair of eyes as she pauses, swings, pauses. Paula looks at her, looks away, sure for a second that the diamond eyes winked at her.

They are holding hands and shuffling together behind the banjos. Paula is grinning broadly, her head dipping from side to side with each shift of her feet. Paula would resemble a person having fun but for the fixed, maniacal widening of her eyes. Daniel wears the self-conscious rictus of a middle-class person trying not to offend the folks. If the empathy control were turned higher, they would both collapse from facial cramps. It is a look that you used to see a lot at presidential campaign time in the days before political candidates had acting coaches and body doubles.

The music stops. The Dervishes continue dancing, most of the crowd applauds itself briefly then laughs. A harsh male voice chants, "Beer break, beer break, can't do the strut without a beer break."

Daniel's smile is fixed, but his eyes are switchblading from side to side, looking at Paula, looking for an exit. Paula's head is still bobbing, her lips tooting the tune. Daniel catches her eye as the beer vendor pushes his way in their direction, makes a cringing gesture toward her, and we zoom in on their heads as they come wonderfully close together.

"I really hate this." His voice is a whisper, his lips just inches from her ear.

Paula turns to him, profile to us, face relaxing into an aspirin commercial portrait of relief. "I'm glad."

Then: Paula and Daniel walking up to a brightly lit café. The sign identifies it as Long's Pig The Barbecue that's got "U" in it

Carefully placed fans pump the smell of tomato, burnt sugar, roast meat and spice into the street. Daniel worries for a second if Paula might be a vegetarian—God would that be dumb—and she licks her lips and smiles.

Paula and Daniel enter, thread their way to the counter at the back. They smile at the giant Polynesian-looking man in pareo and tiki t-shirt. They order two "specials," the ones that come with bibs and mounds of wet napkins. At table, Daniel's first bite sends a rib bone scooting out of his grip, splatting on the table. Drops of sauce splatter them both and they laugh. First date relief laughs—can't worry about looking your best when you're broken out in red sauce pimples.

Daniel dabs at Paula's face with a napkin. He tries to make his touch clinical, it comes off caring. Paula laughs, reaches a finger to his cheek, wipes away a drop and deposits it with a touch on his upper lip. Daniel smiles, suddenly shy, blushes and licks the sauce away.

Two Menus

DINNER AT EMANUEL CARDOSO'S

The Sensitive Guy Course
Pentagrammatical Scallops in Lobster Beurre Blanc
with Salmon Roe and Ossetra Caviar
Belgian White Ale

The Metaphor Course
Asparagus yearning for Pepper-cured Breast of Duck
in a Port and Veal Reduction
Citrus Confetti
Chateau Haut-Brion 1989

The It's Not Dessert Course
Savory Mango Pennants
Chateau d'Yquem 1982

DINNER AT DANIEL FARBER'S

The Sensitive Guy Course
Vegetarian Chili
"My Secret Recipe"
Pierre Celis Texas Hill Country Ale

The Metaphor Course
Grilled Chicken Breast Stuffed with Prosciutto and aged Gouda
Spinach in Olive Oil and Garlic
Couscous Paprikas
Chaddsford Due Rossi

Dessert
Assorted Fruits
Ben & Jerry's Cherry Garcia in a Puff Pastry Basket
Gasparini Brut di Venegazzù

22.

Connie and Cardoso are seated opposite each other on the long ends of a small six-top dinner table, off-white damask cloth. A red rose, its lower stem wrapped in a linen napkin, is beside Connie's plate. Their plates are separated by just a few inches and their wine glasses have overlapped into each other's territory.

Cardoso's back is to the kitchen. They have both worn black and white. Cardoso's shirt has a long-point collar with three-button cuffs. Connie's is silky, open in a thin vee to a spot between her breasts. She has a dusting of makeup on her eyes and her lips are bare. She is reading the menu which Cardoso has printed on a four-by-six-inch card.

The music is a Brandenburg Concerto; it ends and the only sound is the click of a fork on a plate. Connie pulls a scallop away from the pack, it hangs limp and barely cooked; a disk of sea-wet tissue. She waves the scallop under her nose, inhaling, smiling. Tongue meets fork halfway, folds the slice in half, makes a tiny pair of lips that are slowly drawn to the center of her mouth and then disappear.

In profile, her nose is a Semitic Sicilian scythe, her eyes are hazel, predatory, secret-snatching eyes, focused, working, glad to be, knowing-all-about-you-buddy eyes.

Cardoso, pouring beer from a 16 oz. brown bottle. The beer is cloudy, the head is imposing, a lacy white mane.

He stares at the foam, pretends to be studying its fractal complexity. He's really trying to find some words for what she is to him. She is a force of his nature. She is the other half of the broken tile that admits him to the banquet. He wants in and all he has left is faith and maybe this woman.

She knows all about her power and wonders how he got to be like this. She knows she should be careful and she isn't sure what careful is.

Connie blots her lips and reaches for the glass. She brings it to her nose and breaks the silence with a big snorting inhale. Her chest swells, shirt darkens at the nipple spots as her skin presses against the fabric, lightens again. Did you see that? The gesture is feral, wild, sensory leopard dragging off her kill. Unladylike don't ya know.

"Mmmm, wheat beer? Is that coriander? You make it? Here?" In one breath, gestures with her head toward the kitchen.

"Yes, yes, yes and no. I made a batch over at the U-brew with our mutual friend Mr. Long. Each of us ends up with two and a half cases, enough to get us through spring."

"It's really good. You turn the orange rind up a notch?"

"Right, it sets up seafood tastes better."

Connie reaches for another scallop. Cardoso watches her tongue in profile, follows the scallop in.

"Hmm . . . 'Yes, yes, yes.' I like all those yesses in a row, it's got a good beat." She snaps her fingers, yes, yes, yes. Connie has forgotten, or maybe she has ignored his final 'no.' She is smiling, her mouth wide and her lips parted. Her eyes are pointed dead ahead, straight into the future.

"Yes," she says again, maybe just for the pleasure of saying it, and adds the smallest noticeable laugh. To hell with careful.

The plates of Yearning Asparagus come swooping from the kitchen, balanced on Cardoso's hands. He has never been a waiter, but he has watched one or two. He's got the move.

Connie looks at her plate, fingers the menu card by her plate and giggles. No, not giggle, this woman doesn't, couldn't, giggle. It's the special small laugh of someone who hears a very old story cleverly retold. Her laugh is praise for the joker, not the joke.

Her face retreats, arranging itself to hatch some private egg. She glances down to the menu card and then:

"Confetti! I thought maybe you got those stupid Jordan almonds in—"

"Nono, coriandoli . . . È in inglese la carta, no?" And they smile together, leaning back simultaneously in their chairs. Their forks dip to the plates together. No subtitles run beneath their screen.

Cardoso reaches for his plate, forks a slice of duck into his mouth. A drop of the reduction sauce escapes from the fold and runs down his chin. He touches it, touches his tongue, smiling. Connie smiles, squeezing her lips, pointing her smile at the very spot he just touched. She tastes her wine, swirling it in her mouth, chewing on it, parting her lips to draw a breath across it, aerosoling the aroma inside her. She puts the glass down and leaves it and her right hand on Cardoso's side of the table.

"I wondered if that O'Brian of yours was gonna stand up to the duck."

"It doesn't have to stand up to anything really, I just wanted it to hang out, pass the time of, be sociable."

Dishes cleared, table swept of crumbs, Cardoso from the kitchen again, two small plates in his hand. Connie is about to wave him off when he lowers her plate. He has taken a block of mango about an inch square and three inches long. At one end he has carved a 'V.' Then he sliced the block into thin strips, each one looking like a pennant. He threaded a toothpick through the uncut ends to act as a little flagpole and laid four of them out on the plate, the tail of one overlapping slightly the flagpole of the one behind. Looking down on the plate, we see that there is a sprinkling of red dust over the whole composition.

Connie laughs. She picks up a pennant and slides the mango slice off the toothpick and into her mouth. She slurps it in like linguini. For a moment the notched end dangles from her mouth.

Cardoso returns to the kitchen, brings back a half-bottle of honey colored wine. The metal capsule around the top has been cut away and he quickly spins a waiter's corkscrew down into the cork. Two small glasses are filled and Connie eyes her glass but doesn't touch it. She eats the last slice of mango, lingering over it, she seems ready to speak.

Instead of speaking, she takes her glass and stands up, pushes her chair back and walks away from the table to a short couch. The framed picture on the wall behind the couch is of a bottle of 1873 d'Yquem. Connie smiles at the picture and spins herself down onto the couch with her legs extended. Her posture is not exactly come-sit-by-me, but as she leans back she takes a stuffed animal, a long-tailed monkey that had been perched on the couch's back, and tucks it under her arm. She has, you see, a certain langur about her and Cardoso cannot fail to notice.

She sniffs and sips, the taste of honey and apricots washing over her. She closes her eyes and she sees for a second a summer meadow, backlit by a low golden sun, all bees and butterflies. There is perhaps a table-spoon of wine left in her glass and Cardoso approaches her with the bottle.

"Hey Manny, if you drooled a drop of this, would you suck it up like you did that sauce?"

"You bet. Didn't Mozart say something about wine being so precious that not a drop should be wasted?"

"It was Bach, but I know what ya mean." Connie moves the glass away from her face, studies the amount, takes another small sip, tongue tip, flick lip. Studies again, seems to agree to something. She doesn't offer the glass for a refill. Instead she unbuttons one two buttons on her blouse, leans back and pours a dribble of wine between her breasts. She looks down at the wine running, mad with the gravity of the situation.

Cardoso pauses to put the bottle down carefully. She likes him for that. And then he is on his knees beside her, his cheeks brushing the plaquet of her shirt apart. His left hand goes gently to her covered left breast and he rolls her nipple delicately between his index and middle fingers. His tongue is making circles of the spot where the first drops of sauternes landed.

He is in danger of licking her clean when she arches her back and sends a rivulet of d'Yquem down her chest. With balance and muscle she maneuvers a reservoir of sauternes right to her navel, her hand unbuttoning and unclasping and down-pushing the black skirt. She is wearing nothing underneath it.

Cardoso is remembering things he thought he had forgotten. His lips and tongue follow downstream; he stops to nibble and suck an inch of flesh, makes a dry township in Torso County, he moves, he smells the wine and the dark, sharp smell of her. Salty food and good sauternes, my kiddush cup runneth. He flicks his tongue around the rim of what has just become his favorite goblet. Connie arches her back again and the few drops of wine remaining slide down her belly into the tangle of dark black hair tastefully trimmed and Cardoso falls with the drops along her bellydown down.

Somehow, miraculously the music has started again. Brandenburgs. Good Old Don't Waste A Drop Bach. And as the violins kick in, Connie's long soft moan is followed by three sharp indrawn breaths.

23.

Daniel's apartment door opens on a mural, six feet high by three wide. It is a head and shoulders portrait of Timothy Leary. Paula studied him in college and so she steps closer to inspect. The portrait is made up of tiny stamped-ink impressions of Groucho Marx. Paula starts to laugh. As she does, a heaviness that has been sitting on her shoulders disappears. Daniel is startled by the levity, blinded by the lightening, so to speak. He half expects her to dance, and Paula being Paula—a woman who lives up to other people's expectations—she does.

Unbuttoning her coat, she does a little spin and hands Daniel a small black purse. She starts to sing

"Hooray for Captain Spaulding. . ."

Her voice has that same crystal rapture that shined through the madrigal, but now there's a belly laugh in it, a no-condescension, I-love-this-shit humor. One complete turn and Daniel takes the lapel of the coat as it goes by at 16 2/3 rpm and Paula unpeels herself from it as Daniel joins in, hitting the harmony just right.

"The African Explorer,
Did someone call me schnorrer?
Hooray, hooray, hooray."

They laugh, Daniel holding the coat between them as they fall together in a flirty, touched-you-by-accident way. They recover. Paula a little embarrassed that she let herself open the throat so soon. Daniel confused to find himself so far along the intimacy scale so soon. So soon. They draw in breaths to make up for all the breath that they let out. Retreat, recompose. Daniel says his pleonastic "Come in" and carries her coat to a closet off to the left of the mural and into the public side of the apartment facing the street.

Daniel's dining room table is oak and round. From a Public Television program, he learned that a circle is an awkward shape for a romantic dinner, so he has set the places at about ninety degrees from each other.

An easy eye contact, a possible hand touch. His table is partly covered with an American flag crazy quilt.

Paula is wearing a forest green silk shirt buttoned to the throat, black silk slacks and low heels. Her hair, offset nicely by the green of the blouse, is poofed out sideways in red sphinx fashion. Daniel is in plaid button down and khaki.

Two pink candles squat in polished brass candlesticks in the shape of the letter C on the table. On the lower of two oak shelf sideboards, there's a large yellow ceramic airplane. Its fuselage is open at the top and it's carrying a cargo of grapes, baby bananas and lady apples.

"Do you drink beer?" Daniel asks, his head tilted hopefully to the side. His first course is so well knitted together that he has no fall-back position.

"Oh yes, I love beer." Paula is being only partly truthful. The whole truth is that she paid attention to beer when her friends started to. A quick study, she became a maven. A weekly trip to the beer bar at Monk's and she knew all the latest. Then she found that her tips went up because she could recommend newly fashionable beer to her customers. So for pleasure and profit she became a 'chick who digs beer.' She thought about having a t-shirt printed that proclaimed that to the world, but then she thought again.

"Please take a seat, and I'll get the first course"

"Can I help you with anything?"

"No really, that's. . ."

"Oh, let me light the candles . . . do you have any matches?"

"They're in a box on the top shelf, above the fruited plane."

"Above the fruited. . ." and Paula looks at the yellow airplane and laughs again. Back when she had a sense of humor, it was a little like his.

When Daniel was in college, he blushed when his father told him: "If you can make a woman laugh, you can make her come." He wonders if Paula knows this too, knows it with some weird girl-wisdom. The wondering makes him blush again.

Daniel serves his chili in a small white-on-white porcelain bowl on its own service plate. The effect is delicate, it turns the dish away from goober-bubba solid chili. On each service plate, he's balanced a wedge on edge of dense white crustless toast smeared with a cellophane streak of jam. Daniel holds a nearly cylindrical glass at the bottom and pours.

The beer is pale and cloudy with an orange cast. Paula tastes, worried about what she's going to say if she hates the food. She freezes for a second, her eyes flickering down to the dish. She smiles. "Wow, this is really good!"

"Isn't it? I got the recipe from one of those health food store hand-outs, but then I got rid of the beans . . . they were too big and mealy for the rest of the stuff, and I use some quinoa in place, lots of fresh herbs, plum tomatoes . . . I'm glad you like it." Aware of being overly solemn, he smiles his worried primate smile and Paula smacks her lips back at him.

Paula knows about men who love food. She knows what they have, knows why they eat. She's hungry too. The information turns her head, she gets another angle, like walking around a statue. Her stomach dips roller coaster—no, not a coaster, it's a beer mat, steady your self with your hand on your glass. Look up again say hmm. This is really good.

Daniel planned his plate. The chicken breast has been slit to open like a book. The prosciutto and cheese bookmark some middle chapter, close it up, cook it off. Daniel tonged the spinach onto the plates, letting it drain in mid air. He sliced the stuffed chicken into fives and turned the slices so that the layers of meat and cheese faced up and arranged the slices fanned out from the spinach. Sacred heart of chicken, flame-tongued passion in the still white breast. The couscous oozed earth-red at the other end of the sliced chicken breast. Green white red.

Paula's fork speculates with a chicken slice, draws out prosciutto wet with cheese. Daniel's voice, the click of knife. "Hope you like it . . . you must get some pretty great food at work." He sounds thin, tense, reedy and flat like a second date clarinet. Daniel is stuck on food talk, Paula is way beyond him. She is excited and scared. Getting dressed tonight she was nauseated, puke-ready with memory of fumbled love and shame and hurt. Mostly hurt; dizzy-making steel-your-guts hurt. She likes this man. Of course, he makes her sick.

Change the subject, Paula, change your luck. Talk about work, his work. Read from the wallet card that came in the New Year's Resolutions issue of *Mademoiselle*.

"So (say his first name), what's it like being a (his profession here)?"

Daniel's glad she asked. He isn't good at date chat either. He had a vision of himself popping off nervous irrelevancies, dividing his social security number by his shoe size, sharing recipes and comparing quinoa

(KEEN-wha) to couscous and then remembering that couscous was somebody's slang expression for pussy and should he mention that or not? Paula's question saves them both.

"My day job is in TV, I do what they call intellectual property."

"That sounds interesting."

"Mostly it's funny. You know, I send out these letters warning some used car dealer that if he uses Oscar the Grouch in his ads one more time, he's gonna be in trouble. I bet you never thought of Oscar as intellectual anything."

"Well, no. Big Bird maybe. . ."

Daniel feels this hot feeling behind his eyes. He likes this woman.

"Then there's my real job."

"You're a cook?"

"You're too kind. I volunteer for The Child Advocate's Office in City Hall. The advocate speaks up for kids when nobody else will. We're basically lawyers for clients who don't know that they need one." Daniel's voice has changed. It's moved from the front of his face down into his gut. "Mostly we go to court to represent endangered kids, but I'm working on a bunch of different things: Day Camp for Dads and Kids, computer rooms for branch libraries, and of course, the Gun Project."

"Gun Project?"

"Yeah, eleven children have been killed by guns in Philadelphia this year already. and we're not even through March. Last year's total was thirty-one. We're trying to come up with ways to reduce the number of guns in the neighborhoods, but it's tough."

Paula's throat is tight and dry. She knows she's got a going concern here, just not sure which way it's going. "Thirty-one? Kids? Just in Philly?" Her confusion comes out in question marks.

"Yeah, that's just in the city, and this is a low-crime town, safest of the ten biggest cities. We don't even know how many kids were killed by guns in the country last year. Back in '96 the UGA got a law passed that stopped the Centers for Disease Control from even counting the deaths.

"In the meantime, the streets are flooded with guns, kids have guns and they shoot each other. We tried for a law that would make every handgun owner responsible for the legal transfer of his gun . . . you know, if you sell a pistol, you gotta fill out a form saying who you sold it to. UGA was against that, said it amounted to 'registering' guns and

God knows we don't want to do that. Goddamn people love their little bang-bangs more than they love their kids."

Paula has a flash: "little bang-bangs." She's heard that before. But Daniel's lips are pursed, some pissy-mean wave has hit him and she's surfing it. "They own the state legislature, lock, stock and sound bite, so there's no help from the law." He picks up his knife, moves his chicken a quarter-inch to the right. The charm has gone out of him.

"Some days I just come home and cry."

Paula doesn't know what to do with this. She's not sure if she's ever heard a man say that sometimes he cries, she's sure she never heard it on a date. She runs her fork in meditative circles around her spinach. She looks down at her plate, lifts a bite of couscous that vibrates bright red on her fork as if it were trying to escape into another dimension.

Second date seduction just went out the door, the room is clear. Two people left, blinking like they just woke up. Paula feels a new fear now, different than the one she got dressed with. She can't screw him and not tell him what she does when she goes jogging, and she's afraid to screw him and she wants so much to tell him. Oh Tom, goddamn you for dying. If she tells him, he will own her, have her. Her fears—the ones about men and their cocks and guns—will mean nothing. If she tells him, she'll be more naked than she ever feared.

She thinks these things and she looks at Daniel, seeing the music of the man. Smelling his tune, feeling the thump, the rhythm of his words. She has an ear for music, she makes a choice.

Paula rocks back in her chair, says to Daniel, "There's something I'd like to tell you." She looks like one of those girl gymnasts about to make a run at the vaulting horse, scared, determined and what-the-fuck. Daniel wonders if he's just blown it, thinks that what she has to say is about him. He straightens up over a big belly expansion, a Buddhist breath, equal to good or evil chance.

The right angle of their place setting is squished a little now by Daniel's sliding his chair towards her and by Paula's pivot, feet pressing down on the side stretcher of her chair.

Paula tells him. She tells him something, Tom's story at least: the man, the shot, the trial, the little sister. He takes it all. In. He listens the way she always wanted Tom to listen, picking up little bits of her feeling and pressing them against the puzzle pieces of his own. Something fits, he keeps it.

She tells him about the ad and the senator and the UGA and the anger. She uses the word 'violated' then she uses the word 'rape.' Daniel winces at the worst parts, leans in, nodding as she tells more. He reminds her suddenly of a fighter, gloves up, c'mon baby give me more. The corners of his mouth are pulled up and he's just barely nodding in rhythm to her words. She tells him about seeing gun images everywhere, about the little raised arms in car windows. And then she stops. She can't look at his face anymore, it's too good and it makes her want to keep on talking. She looks away, to the candle holders: the two Cs on opposite ends of the table, candles burned way down. From C to shining C.

"I want to tell you something, client-to-lawyer. Deepest confidence. May I?"

"Yes. Please."

And so she tells him about the magazines and how she started to love what she started out to hate. How the guns seemed so strong just when she seemed so weak. She wants to tell him about waiting for the UPS truck and about practicing hitting the same target over and over.

She'd like to tell him about shooting as many windshields as she could find on Valentine's Day because she was sure she would get caught and she wanted to bag her limit before the police hauled her off. She wants to say how good it felt and how much stronger she was afterward.

And she doesn't. Too soon. Bad enough to let the hurt out. "Tell me about Tom," Daniel says, and she's glad.

Paula and Daniel are crunched together on a couch a few steps from the table. Their dessert plates are puddles of melting purple with ruined towers, puff pastry ziggurats. A banana peel is folded neatly between their plates. Did they share the banana, or would they have choked with laughter if they did? The candles have burned to stubs and out. She's asleep, leaning slouching into his shoulder, a knitted throw wrapped around her. A swatch of bright red hair is sprouting between her head and his chest and her hand has dropped loosely on his leg. He is still upright, homo completely erectus, arm around her.

In the window behind them, the pink of the street light goes out and the shadow of the ginkgo tree almost disappears from the brick wall across the street. Then a subtler, cooler shadow begins to form at a lower angle.

Dawn.

24.

The room is dark except for the beacon of Paula's TV set and the light that bounces off the wall behind the bed.

Below the incandescent screen, two lumps, two mountains-in-coverland. One mountain moves toward the other which leans away from it and then, not too reluctantly, allows itself to be stroked. A third mountain, larger than the first two, jerks its way over and ducks behind the first one. There is a burrowing motion and the first peak pulls itself away and then eases back.

This tectonic dance happens in irritating obscurity. The light from the TV, whose image shows a car driving an impossibly scenic road, is washing over everything, making outlines too hot to look at, shadows too dark to see.

SHAZAM! Her feet. Those are feet. Paula's feet under the covers, another foot in her bed. Tickle. Paula has a lover. Is it Daniel? Is it Cardoso? Is it the waitress from Odetta?

Stay.

Tuned.

Onscreen, there's a pub: a U-shaped mahogany bar with its closed end pointed to the camera, two upholstered armless barstools on either side of the U, a Chippendale back bar. Standing behind the bar in a vertically striped shirt and suspenders is a man, forty-five years old and slightly handsome. Just behind him on the right of the screen are three brass tap handles. On his left is the handle of an old fashioned hand-pumped beer engine, the sort that draws cask-conditioned ale from the cellar. The man turns to the taps, he has an empty pint glass in hand. He pours expertly, the glass filling slowly. Paula admires his technique.

The picture, which had been in snowy black and white, begins to sharpen. The glass is filling, luminous chestnut-brown. The developing head is medium beige.

While the barkeep is pouring, a voice off stage is saying,

"Welcome to THE OUTRAGEOUS BAR & GRILL with Nick Blaylock, the late night talk show from the other side of the ocean and the far side of the moon. And now, here's Nick Blaylock. . ." Paula loves this show, she thinks of the host as Prickly Nicky, the difficult man of her dreams. Nick takes a small beer mat from under the bar and tosses it casually in the air. As it falls, it hits the edge of his glass, then his fist, then his outstretched pinky and finally lands flat on the bar by his left elbow. With perfect concentration, he aims his glass at the mat, makes a landing, looks up and smiles.

"I've been reading the paper today—I love American newspapers— and I saw an interesting pair of items." His accent is British, U-shaped like the bar. He pronounces 'been' like 'bean' which does, we must admit, make the word sound more important, less an auxiliary, more a verb.

He fetches a folded newspaper from under the bar, a pair of wire rims from his breast pocket inboard of the suspender and begins to read. "In Silverton, Nevada, this morning a man named Jesse Howard bought a semi-automatic shotgun at a yard sale. Now for those of you from outside the U.S., I should explain that a yard sale is an event in which an American family clears out their closets, attics and cellars, gathers up all the accumulated oddments of their lives—outgrown bicycles, broken toasters, used engagement rings, things like that—and deposits them on the lawn in front of their house. Then the neighbors come round, buy the detritus, cart it home and store it in their closets, attics and cellars." Studio audience laughs. Paula, who loves to browse through the stuff at sidewalk sales, is a little embarrassed.

"So this chap bought a semi-automatic shotgun at . . . eh? What's that? Oh yes, of course . . . for those of you watching from outside gun-land, a semi-automatic gun is one that fires just as fast as you can pull the trigger. The exploding gases of each fired missile somehow jockey the next one into position to be fired. No wasted motion and so forth." He pronounces the word 'miss aisle,' which makes a bullet sound rather harmless.

"In any event, he got some ammunition with his purchase—bullets of the sort used to hunt elk—and he drove to the local branch of something called Burger Worker. For those of you outside the States, well, never mind, perhaps you're better off. In any event, he went to the counter carrying his new gun and . . . um, yes . . . I quote: 'Seventeen-year-old Jennifer Knight asked Mr. Howard if she could help him. In reply,

Mr. Howard raised his gun and shot Ms. Knight in the face. The high school senior, who was planning to attend Brigham Young University in the fall and study nursing, died instantly. The manager of the store, a Mr. Jeffrey Knight (no relation) rushed to the sound and was killed by a blast to the chest. Mr. Howard then turned around to see a dozen or so people scrambling for the door or for cover. Shooting apparently at random, he killed three more people and injured an additional eight. Among the dead were a Ms Sarah Greenstein, a teacher at a nearby elementary school and her eleven-year-old daughter Natalie. Also killed was eleven-year-old Kelly Young who was having an after-school snack with the Greensteins.'"

Someone in the TV studio audience laughs. Mr. Blaylock, who has become serious in spite of himself, looks up over his glasses in the direction of the laughter. "That's not," he says, "the funny part. Did you see the laugh sign light up? Hardly!" His words are drama, his timing pure comic. There is a tiny ripple of laughter in response to this misdirection play and then the ice pack settles back on everyone's gut and there is quiet.

Nicky plays the silence, two heartbeats, three, takes a sip, turns a page. "Now here's another tale of violence. Last weekend it seems that a gang of conspirators in Philadelphia, Pennsylvania, and its suburbs, went hunting for windscreen stickers. Those are those charming little decalcomania that announce to the world that you're a vegetarian or that you heart your Chihuahua and so forth. It seems that the ones they prized were the not-too-rare emblems of the United Gun Association. Again, for our viewers in the rest of the world, the UGA, as it's called, is an organization that promotes gun ownership in the U.S. and fiercely resists any attempts to restrict it.

"In any event, when these urban big game hunters found their quarry, they shot them with a type of toy rifle that uses compressed air to fire little pellets. In the process, of course, many UGA-owned windscreens went down to dark death." "Now here's the part that I like . . . In Washington today, Senator Warren Cole of Nevada called a press conference. He wanted to denounce an outrage and he wanted to call for legislation. He wanted to express his horror, in no uncertain terms ladies and gentlemen, at this wanton and senseless loss of—windshields." Studio audience groans. "Better hurry down to Burger Worker, Senator"

Nick folds his paper, rests it on the bar, peels off glasses.

92 ■ LYNN HOFFMAN

"Our guests tonight are some veterans of sexual abuse who don't want to be called 'victims' and get this, a racial refugee. We'll be back after this message."

Paula throws off the covers and jumps to the set. She is naked in the cathode light. As she reaches to turn the set off she turns toward the one in the bed. The back light of the set bounces along her belly, catches the tangle of pubic hair, gives an outline to her breast. "I have to turn this off now, it's late," she says, but her voice is trembling. She is shivering naked, the room is warm.

Before she can turn the power off, a figure rises from the left side of the bed and crawls to her. It is the quick pudgy shape of Daniel that stretches a hand, his full lips that she sees in profile as he says, "No, it's not late. It's something else isn't it? Come here and tell me about it."

As the TV light disappears, he can barely see to urge her back to her pillow. "No," she says, "I can't, I. . ." And there's the sound of flesh slipping on flesh, of arms around shoulders, of bodies aligning and face rustling chest hairs. There is a chance here to be taken and Paula, as if she were watching a stranger, sees herself take it.

"There's something I have to tell you."

"Something else?"

"Yes."

There is a sound like a sob and a hushing, then whispers and ummhmms of rage and understanding and acceptance and plans being made and then the gentle dark.

25.

The people inside Bethany Baptist Church seem anxious, awkward, in their places and out of place. As a rule, they come here to celebrate or be soothed, to wrap themselves in the holy and to touch God and let him touch back. They are church-going people and this place is theirs, but today they are not quite at home. There is no patting of sleeves, no bobbing of heads, no little winks and grins.

Today there is desolation, they are gathered for a funeral. Beneath the grief, there is horror and it hangs from the walls and clings to the benches. The tiny white coffin in the front of the church holds the body of seven-year-old Michelle Cutner, shrouded in the blue and white tartan uniform of the St. Martin de Porres School. Four days ago, Michelle was with her mom and sister buying peanut butter candy in the variety store on the corner of 20th and Christian. It was the last day of school before Easter vacation. Michelle saw her friend Jasmine walking by the store and went out to join her. The two first-graders started to walk east on Christian towards 19th. They walked past the vacant lot next to the variety store, waved to Jasmine's sister who was sitting on a stoop across the street in the sunshine of the first warm day of spring.

Six doors down from that stoop, Ronald McGovern was standing in his half-open doorway, shouting into the street. The sixteen-year-old boy was yelling at a friend of his who was lounging against a car. Ronald wanted his friend to drive him a few blocks south to a playground. He had been in a fight there just a few minutes before. Ronald wanted to find the boy he fought with and "fuck him up." Ronald's friend wasn't in a driving mood, so Ronald drew a .22 caliber Ruger KP-4 pistol from his back pocket and fired a shot, originally intended for playground use, at his friend. The bullet missed the friend and struck Michelle in the side and spattered Jasmine with her blood. The little girl lay on the sidewalk, licking her lips, her eyes wide and staring, until the paramedics arrived.

They took Michelle to Children's Hospital where she was pronounced dead at 3:36 pm.

The mourners who can bear to think about what has happened are struck in the side themselves, blinded silent by it. The rest are quiet with the effort to not see.

Organ music trails off, and a man walks to the pulpit. He is carrying a small soft-bound black book, his finger marking a page. The man is short and bald. He is The Reverend Telly Henderson, forty-eight years old.

He has a mildness, a clarity about him. He looks like a preacher who breathes heaven, whose home may already be there. He tries to speak, his lips move, no sound comes out. He pinches the edges of his eyebrows, head down. Then,

"My dear brothers and sisters, I hope you will forgive me. I have no prayer in my heart right now. I hope God will forgive me.

"Young Michelle, who we are saying good-bye to today, played with my daughter in front of this church. Many of you knew her, a happy little tomboy climbing on fences and running, always running in the streets.

"I . . . I. . ." He stumbles. This is not a failure of rhetoric, there is a crack forming in a solid soul and something is leaking out. "I know that the timing of life and death is in the hands of the Lord. I know that the Christian offers up his pain as a sacrifice in honor of the sacrifice made for us on Calvary. What chokes my prayer today is not Michelle's death. It is the monstrous evil that has overtaken us and killed her."

He pauses, looks up, his chest heaves in short breaths. He continues in a voice that does not soar above the congregation, but grinds its way to them through the stones beneath their feet.

"Our streets are flooded with guns—guns like the one that killed her. When we try to get the guns from our streets, from our lives, we are told that the law protects the guns. We are told that there are people who like to hunt and play with guns and who don't feel safe without their guns. They worry, we are told, that if you take away Ronald McGovern's gun, the next thing we'll do is sneak into their safe suburban houses and try to take away theirs.

"They say that freedom's price is the necessity of owning guns, any guns. What they don't say is that the price of all these guns is being paid today by seven-year-old girls on their way home from school.

"Not too many years ago there were groups of people willing to make us pay the price for their feeling safe and good. They were called the KKK, the Ku Klux Klan. From 1865 to 1957, the Klan was responsible for the lynching deaths of over 9000 black people in this country. Last year, the guns so lovingly protected by the United Gun Association, killed 3,000 black people. Five children a week are killed by guns. It took the Klan, with their ropes and their torches almost a century to do what the UGA accomplishes with its lawyers and lobbyists every three years."

He draws in a sharp breath through his nose. The snuff of indignation has pushed him across some spiritual boundary. Where will he go from here?

"It was this monster as much as any demons in Ronald McGovern that took Michelle from us. It used to be the KKK who sowed the seeds of death among us, today it is the UGA. We fought the KKK and we won. We stood up for justice and our courage brought us allies and all of us with God's blessing slew that old monster. Do we have the courage to fight again today? I pray to the living God that we do.

"Dear Lord, ignite us with your spirit. Let the flames of passion for goodness rise up and consume the monster that threatens our children. Comfort us that the life of this little girl shall not have been lost in vain. Turn us away from despair and towards the light. In Jesus' name. Amen."

The congregation amens him back, a soft breathy amen of relief. They were praying for his soul and it seems that their prayers have been answered.

And having prayed, the Reverend Henderson is animated again. He opens his prayer book and begins to read from the 23rd Psalm of David.

"The Lord is my shepherd, I shall not want. . ."

26.

So there. She told him. Told this new boyfriend, first realreal lover. Told him about her pellet gun and about what she really did when she ran. And even though he kissed her softly in the morning when he left, she was sick with her stupid self. It could spoil everything.

She felt ashamed and afraid. She could almost feel the shame and the fear sitting on her shoulders, like two little devils, forks poking at a spot in the middle of her chest.

Sometimes, running hard enough and long enough, she could run away from them. Exercising her demons, she called it as she sat on her stoop and strapped on the plastic boots of her new roller blades. Kick her legs and swing her arms and concentrate on staying upright. Forward progress, she says.

P.O.'D IN THE DELAWARE VALLEY

"*Good afternoon and welcome to P.O.'d in the Delaware Valley, the show that brings you ordinary people getting it off their chests. Today, people from around the Delaware Valley and around the country let you know what's bugging them.*"

The logo in TV format shows a leprechaun shaking his fist at the lower half of a giant. The voice is offscreen and enthusiastic, British and slightly accusatory.

"*Tonight's top story concerns a group of inner-city Philadelphia residents who left a funeral to do some mourning in the suburbs.*" *Note false note. This is an out-of-town broadcast. People in Philadelphia call it by neighborhoods, don't have no 'inner city.'*

The film shows a mostly brown crowd walking in a conventional protesters' oval on a mostly white street.

There is a small girl, six years old with a sign that says Who killed my friend? *The camera lowers and lingers on her, killing her friend again somehow or lunching on the body. The half-bodies of the adults ripple behind her. Other signs say* Guns Kill Kids, Michelle's Death Won't Even Count, *and* Pistols Don't Make Peace. *A woman, shuffling and unsteady in a bright pink coat, has a sign that says,* Senator Santacci Voted for the Gun That Killed My Daughter.

Then the phony voice-over: "*When little Michelle Cutner was gunned down on a Philadelphia street, her family, friends and neighbors decided to express their sadness by protesting against guns in their neighborhood. So they boarded a bus to the suburban offices of United States Senator Jim Santacci. The Senator, who received substantial Support from the United Gun Association in his last campaign, led the fight in the Senate against a bill that would have required the registration of all privately owned handguns. He was the author of a 1996 bill that stopped the Centers for Disease Control from counting the number of children killed by guns in the country.*" *The whining accent from some bad neighborhood in the Empire sticks to us like a leech, sucking out compassion, pumping back a formula smugness in its place. Toxic flush in the cheeks, you can stand it, might grow to like it, voice goes on.*

"*Led by Michelle's pastor, the Reverend Telly Henderson, the mourners made the long trip to ask the representative why he had voted the way he did. When Reverend Henderson knocked on the senator's office door, an aide* told him that Santacci was not available. Reverend Henderson then asked the aide to join him in a prayer for the soul of Michelle Cutner. The aide shut the door."

Shot of the reverend looking leaner and farther away than last we saw him. Quick pan of the crowd behind him, there's a white face or two among the brown, one of them is Daniel. The one-second close-up shows him with an eyebrow arched, face a restrained prophetic angry mask. Give him a Rock of Ages and he'd likely throw it.

Back to a close-up of Reverend Henderson. There is the hint of a cheek-bone, a downdrop wrinkle at the corner of his eye. He is with us, in this world, got his ticket punched, paid for the trip.

27.

Sticky, misty fog softens the edges of her street as Paula comes down the steps of her stoop. Her stocking feet stick lightly to the damp concrete steps. Daniel follows her. She is wearing urban camouflage, a stained, concrete-gray sweat shirt, frayed black-top tights and olive drab back pack. Her hair is tucked up in a watch cap. Her face is luminously pale. If she fell to the curb on the right day, she could pass for trash and be hauled away. She looks up, rolls her face in the light mist, judges it to be a trifle and straps on her skates. The skates look new. Paula skates to the theater district, wondering why she didn't think of this before. Cover more ground, leave the scene faster. Daniel skates half a block behind her. They time it just right, everything is letting out at once.

No great surprise; not a lot of decals in the crowd around the Orchestra. Paula skates over to the Philadelphia Opera Theater. Nobody showing the colors at T-pot either, although the Opera crowd looks a little more comfortable with ordnance than the Orchestra folks.

In front of the Bellevue at Broad and Walnut, a knot of moviegoers is yakkin' and chattin' and heading for the bus. Two more blocks to the road show of Miss Saigon—Paula, down Walnut Street against traffic, weaving through the wet air and the barely moving cars, watching the crowds leave the theater. The Commonwealth of Pennsylvania Drug Dispensary is closed, but there's an afterimage of a few leftover junkies who are as happy where they are as they would be anywhere else. There are also a dozen or so junky boys and girls apprenticing on corners, filterfeeding, begging through the crowd, learning to ignore the light chill of the air, looking for the big cold inside. They are too young for the Commonwealth drugs, the street is too well patrolled for stealing.

A bare-chested kid wearing a pink jockstrap over army surplus wool pants is singing "Memory." He is glazed with mist. His companion, a girl who looks to be about fourteen, is wearing dirty white tights and a white t-shirt with clumsy stripes hand painted. She pirouettes around him mechanically, her body gradually exposing itself as the mist soaks through her costume. She is shaking a white foam soda cup, offering it with a flourish to the passing crowd. Paula skates out into the street, reverses, goes with the grain, reading windshields, checking the crowd.

The cars are barely moving. In front of Big Beef, she sees a double. A blue Dodge Neon, left lane, UGA decal in rear window, Santacci for Senator bumper sticker just left of the license plate. Quick scan, no cop nearby, alley just a few yards away, be gone in ten seconds. Perfect.

Paula feels a hard heat in her chest as her right hand goes marsupial, in the pouch, on the gun. She slows down, waiting, angling the ricochet toward straight up, car horn bronks impatiently, muzzle shows. Click, smack, good shot.

Paula leans right to skate around the passenger side when the door swings open, catching her and trapping her between it and a car in the right lane. A seat belt half whips out as a man's hand grabs her shirt. She feels something more like disgust than fear, and she screams, spitting the taste of his touch back at him. The grabber pulls his hand back for the second it takes her to stumble a few steps backward. She spins on her skates and he is out of the car and running at her. As she reaches the curb, he grabs her shirt from behind and Paula fights for her balance, arms and skates looking for consensus.

Daniel, half a block away, skates to her furiously, heavily. Paula is making way, spinning as she's being pulled into the arms of the passenger, a medium-sized man in a shiny red jacket. He has one hand on her, then two, her legs still pushing. They are both on the sidewalk now, Paula struggling for enough breath to make a scream.

Suddenly, a small patent leather shoe catches the man behind his knee. His leg folds, the point of an umbrella thunders down to catch him along the ear.

Voices, bellowyells. "Police! Pervert!"

Young junky boys buzz over to the fuss, looking for a loose wallet, a little theft, something to talk about. Paula recovers with a frightened over-the-shoulder look. She starts to skate toward the alley but the car's driver has popped out from the other side and he's in action too, face red, blood pumping. ". . . my fuckin' car will ya . . ." He has a better shot than his buddy did, approaching Paula from the right, perpendicular to her best path out of there.

She sees him, skates left away from him and toward the building

line and away from the safety of the alley. Now she'll have to try her
luck among the pedestrians, hoping that nobody wants to be a volunteer crimestopper. She raises her hand to catch the wall just as Daniel
appears from the left and smacks into the second man. Blindsided, the
man falls forward and Daniel lands on him and then slides to the pavement.

The providential shoe and shout belong to Lichtmann, Cardoso's
Urban Ranger, his voice raucous as a gull's. He's standing above the man
in red who is kneeling on the pavement holding his ear. A cop arrives
"What's going on here, Mr. Lichtmann?"

"Officer, I'd like to make out a complaint." ID's flashed. "Would you
be good enough to radio Captain Beagles? I believe he's on duty somewhere in the area."

Radio static, more cops, ". . . apparently trying to molest that young
woman . . . must have frightened her to death." Lichtmann again ". . .
and then the second hooligan slammed into this poor fellow who was
quietly skating down the street, apparently intending to sexually assault
him too." The car which had been left driverless, is seen pulling away, a
young cop at the wheel.

We hear "impoundment . . . right to remain silent . . . are you all right
there buddy?" as Daniel is lifted and brushed.

Paula has rounded a corner on Sansom Street. Keeping her fear
tucked away, she pulls an improbable flowered voile skirt out of her
back pack, snaps it around her waist, velcroed in place. She slips the
backpack off, folds the gun, sweatshirt and stocking cap inside it. Paula
shakes out her hair and turns slowly on her skates; a handsome young
woman, whimsically dressed. An actress maybe, going home after the
show.

On the way home, she sees a police car in front of Daniel's stoop.
She raises her toe and drags the skate's brake along the blacktop. A uniformed cop is getting out and steadying a shaky Daniel across the sidewalk and up the steps and Paula's eyes are wet as she skates on home.

Daniel is lying in bed, t-shirt and underpants, ice pack on his knee. Some scrape marks have been wiped clean and we see the beginnings of bruising and swelling. Paula is sitting at his foot, stripped to ratty black tights and jog bra. Her hand is on his shin, wanting to soothe, afraid to hurt.

Daniel's face is set, his eyes focused on some spot offscreen. His bedroom has become, ever so slightly, their bedroom, and now, in this shared space, he has to explain himself.

He is composed, warlike, a man ready to say something dangerous. What he says is, "I can't do things like this." He turns his head a few degrees to see Paula. There is no hint in his voice of a man asking permission. This is what's so, he says.

There is a long silence. Paula is reading his face, gets to the end of his chapter. "It's the law, isn't it?" she says.

"Yes. I believe in law. If I keep on doing things like we did tonight, I lose everything. Even my power to help you. I'm sorry, but that's it. I'm not afraid of violating the law, I'm afraid of . . . well, violating me. I wouldn't tell you what to do, but for what it's worth, the real power isn't in popping windshields."

Paula wants to meet his truth with another one just as brave. She turns away from him.

"I love you," she says without moving or signaling for an embrace, her voice clear and pledge-of-allegiance bland, reading the directions off the box, this is so for her, no reply needed. There.

Daniel's face trembles, his eyes stay softly fixed on her. He smiles and moves his hands to her. He will wait, make his case later. He turns her shoulder so she faces him. The flash of light on the cheek nearest him is, no doubt, a tear.

Paula's eyes have a flash of their own. She is noticing that the big, firecracker moments don't absorb her self as fully as the storybooks said they might. She is learning, with just a touch of regret, that you can say "I love you" to someone for the first time and a part of your brain can be attached at that very moment to the hot sexy feeling of doing something bad and not getting caught. She wishes that it weren't so, but she has to admit it, gotta tell the truth. Crime has made an honest woman of her.

28.

In front of us, the Ben Franklin Parkway points toward City Hall. Our park bench lets us see past Rodin's fame-slain Thinker, sucking his knuckles at the entrance to the Rodin Museum. In the distance, in the thin, late winter sunshine, we observe a swaying dark blob that widens and narrows without changing height. The blob becomes a group of six skaters, telephotically compressed. The widening is the centrifugal swaying as they saw their way up the street. They are dressed in black tights and black windbreakers. Their helmets are black and they are wearing sunglasses. A team.

As they come closer we see faces, skin, pale, several shades of brown, a dark pale, a copper, a whiter shade of pale.

Closer. These are all women skaters, admirably legged. They are moving easily, playfully, switching positions in the pack, laughing. They pass the museum and the lead pair checks the light, takes the ramp down and off the sidewalk. The other four fly off the curb and land with flexi-knees. They cross the street, remount the curb and we watch them, black molded butts pushing back the concrete.

At the gilded statue of Joan of Arc they lean and swing and slow and with big easy gliding movements push to a brown van whose side door is open for them. They skate up, first two then four and step up into the van. Jackets pop off, skates stay on, door closes, van pulls away. In a few minutes, the van arrives at the stadiums in the south end of the city. There is a parking lot full of cars around one of them and the brown van enters, follows a pointing arm, turns right, then left then left again and heads to the back of the lot, toward the active, growing edge of the carmass.

Then it stops in the middle of a line of cars, the sliding door on the side away from the street and the attendants. Six figures pop out.

The skaters are dressed now in motley; gray plaid and brown checks and faded orange: the team colors have changed to Mud and Compost.

They turn without stopping for bearings, fanning out, metastasizing over the lot. Last one out shuts the door and the van moves slowly, as if looking for a spot where the iron law of parking says that none can be.

One skater trails long black hair behind her helmet and down the yoke of her plaid shirt. She is lumped, anamorphic and thick in loose denim trousers. Across her shoulder is a khaki web belt. As she skates, the belt climbs up her back and in answer a pouch drops at her side. She drags a zipper and her hand goes inside the pouch. With her hand in place, she slows her skating and makes big sweeps of her head with each leg pump. Six strides, seven, she slows a little more, wheels and points her head, then her hand, then the pouch. We follow her line of sight. Yes, red blue gold raised arm clutching rifle, LIFE MEMBER, thack-whack crack spin and skate on girl.

Big picture. The van has reached the end of the land of cars. It stops, seems to count, slowly turns around and heads back to the entrance. As it does we can just make out little points of motion in long swoops and tight curves, combing the lot, pointing fat bags, picking nits, then falling toward a spot where the van seems to be heading. Two minutes after it turns around, the van stops and—run the tape backwards, mama—six skaters disappear inside it. At the exit, the driver waves her hand but doesn't slow down, the attendants barely turn from their ticket selling and pointing. In a minute the van is heading north on Broad Street and even through the darkened windows, a passerby could see the slapping of upraised hands and the constrained bounciness of seat-belted hugs.

http://www.americanaryanmovement.com

Sieg Heil!
Welcome to the American Aryan Movement Home Page
Vol. 16, No. 3, March 2006

Don't trust the UGA. As patriotic gun owners are becoming aware of the Jewish leadership of the gun-bashing movement, the United Gun Association has continued pandering to these parasites. Through the pages of Guns and Ammo Magazine, they have been perpetuating the lie that Germany's National Socialist Government confiscated guns.

The truth is that German law (Waffengesetz) allowed German citizens to own and carry firearms—Jews, of course, were not German citizens. The law was not completely on target; it required a permit (Waffenwerbschein) to buy a handgun and a second license (Waffenschein) was required to carry a handgun in public. No law was required for long gun ownership.

The law irritated the Jews because it excluded them from the firearms business, but it certainly did not aim to prevent the ownership or use of firearms. Despite these facts, there are some who support Second Amendment rights who have fallen for the Jewish trick of associating gun-grabbing with Hitler. These people say things like, "The first thing Hitler did when he came to power was round up all the guns." Such statements, when they are made by a person who supports the Second Amendment, reveal the person's ignorance or dishonesty. When they are made by Jews, it is clear they intend to deflect blame from their fellow Jews.

GUNNING SCARED. In another example of gutlessness on the blight wing, members of the UGA have had their vehicles attacked in a cowardly and systematic way that has the smell of Jewishness all over it. The petty criminals involved have been shooting at window stickers that proclaim UGA membership. The weapon of choice? A BB gun!

The attacks began in Philacreamcheesedelphia in January and have spread around the East Coast. There has even been an attack in the once solid German city of St. Louis. So far the UGA response has been—silence!

Imagine that. The mighty, patriotic UGA, 3 million members strong, silenced by BB guns wielded by Jews.

It's time for true American Patriots to remember who the real enemy is. Don't support organizations that traffic with the enemy!

Don't even recognize organizations that are afraid of him! Free the Land of Impurities! Have A Nice Day!

membership information

book and insignia catalog

29.

A woman walks down a law office sort of hallway and into an elevator. She is thirty or so, the youth obviously brushed off her, replaced with something harder but not yet brittle. Average height, average looks, average average. Elevator stops, red LED sign flashes: STATE YOUR NAME. Sara Arkwright speaks, doors open. When Sara steps out of the elevator, she's in a fluorescent room deep in UGA headquarters, shadowless light coming from everywhere: walls, floors, ceilings, all cells in the photobelly of the beast.

The conference table is glass-topped on steel legs. Light from the floor passes through the glass, making cheekbone shadows that hide the eyes and make the faces of the three seated men seem monstrous and skeletal. It's the old flashlight under the chin effect.

The man at the head of the table is tall and athletic looking: fiftyish, crew cut, veiny red nose, grey eyes. He's wearing a tan suit, white shirt, yellow tie. There is a rosette in his lapel and a pile of printed material at his elbow.

On his right is a chubby, red-faced, sandy-haired man in a plaid jacket. There is a cigarette burning in a glass ashtray at his right elbow, the smoke rising in almost a straight line to the ceiling.

Across from him, a thin dark man is leaning into the table, his hands folded and his eyes off in middle distance. He is badly but earnestly dressed in a clean dark suit that ripples over his surface.

Seeing the three from the far end, she makes them for a moment more bestial than skeletal in the weird light. From the left, Sara notes the pig, the ferret and the hawk.

Sara takes the fourth seat at the table, to the right of the porcine man and in front of a yellow legal pad. She bites her lower lip and displaces a trace of lipstick.

From her seat at the head of the table, she looks down its length at a standing young man in a shapeless white shirt. His wholesomeness is partly an illusion of contrast: the shadow cast by a large personal computer keeps him out of the ghoulish underlighting.

"Miss Arkwright." The man at the head of the table greets her with a flicker of his eyes and a small head bounce. "This young man is from research. We have a presentation here that we'd like you to see . . . we'll be formulating a response." Another head bounce reinforced with an eyebrow arch in the direction of the young man from research.

The white-shirted man begins. "Early this year in Philadelphia, a gang of vandals went on a rampage, attacking vehicles displaying our insignia. In every case, windows were broken and air rifle ammunition was found in many of the cars. The attacks got some play in the media and copycat criminals started copying. Which is what they do. Ahmm."

His hand moves to a button on the table that's connected by a cord to the computer. "This graph shows the number of attacks per month."

"No it doesn't." the porky man interrupts. "That screen is completely blank."

The young man turns the computer to him as if it were a reluctant dance partner. You are going to tango, goddammit! He squeezes the end of the cord in his hand, punches a combination on the keyboard, types something, squeezes again. There is sweat. The screen remains blank.

"I don't understand . . . it worked this morning." His face is sucked into itself in a parody of pain. Betrayed, just like that time in high school when . . .

"Thank you, that will be all, you can leave that here." The hawk speaks quickly, no body language but his eye-flick towards the door. As the boy steps back, the weird light reaches him and he looks, for just a second, like a tiny white skull. All that's left of him is the click.

"You know what's been going on." It is, of course, the ferret at the head of the table. "This windshield breaking thing has gone from an annoyance to a real ball-buster. We look stupid . . . worse than that, we look weak. It's showing up in membership. What that little fella would have told us is that new memberships are down forty-four percent from the same month last year. Life memberships, the real endowment-making, salary-stuffing ones, are off more than half. Worse yet, non-renewals have tripled! Fucking tripled!"

He is moved. He leans forward, forearms on the table edge, finger drilling into the glass top. Tripled non-renewals does it.

"What that adds up to gentlemen," his eyes survey the room, taking

Sara in with the gentlemen and without irony, "is that we are experiencing a net negative growth.

"It gets worse. Now there's competition. Nothing serious yet, but it's out there. Something called the American Sporting Federation . . . hunters, fisherman, conservationists . . . they're taking ads on T.V. and they only support long guns! No pistols, no assault weapons. Look at this."

He slides a brochure from the pile beside him and spins it on the table in front of him. We catch it as it slows down. There is a photograph of a pistol with an X Drawn through it with a brush. The caption below says Nothing Sporting About It.

"There's more, lots more, a rumor that IACP is going to announce a partnership with HCI in an ad and legislative information program."

Sara translates to herself from Washingtonese: InterAmerican Association of Chiefs of Police, Handgun Control Incorporated.

"Ouch." It's the fat man. "So the next thing you know you've got uniformed cops showing up in the congressman's office lobbying for ammunition restriction or some damned thing and then there's a photo op and some creep that we've bought and paid for three times over is voting against us."

"Don't give 'em any fuckin' ideas, pardon my French. I'm not even going to tell you about 'Nuns Hate Guns' or any of the real wing-nut militia stuff. The point is that we're being hit from all sides and we need ideas, I mean BIG ideas. Sara, it would be best if you took some notes, you're going to be a very busy little lady over the next few weeks. The first thing is that I want to know who started this. Hire that fancy detective agency, the one we use for Senators. And have them report directly to me."

Sara smiles at him, nods. She's thinking, "little lady? schmuck! you're such a schmuck." She learned the word from a guy she dated who did publicity for the Sierra Club. The word means "penis" but it signifies "idiot." She likes the word, finds it handy, emphasizes the "shhh" when she says it.

The third man, the hawk, who has been silent until now, jerks at a wrinkle in his lapel. He speaks without looking at anyone else in the room. "Maybe we shouldn't do anything."

The boss ain't buying it. "We have to do something. We're being beaten up all over the country by nuns and roller bladers and . . . and people with BB guns fer chrissake!"

"I understand. It's bad, but what I'm saying is maybe we should just keep on doing what we're doing and let these people make fools out of themselves. They've got to go too far, it's just a matter of time. White people never know when to stop. You can count on it."

The room is quiet except for the fluttering sound of a good idea that never stood a chance expiring on the table. Sara scribbles and the computer in the corner makes a sudden, incontinent hum.

Cardoso's Diary 6
....

"Well I was black-tied to the steak and baked potato with Lucius last night."

The voice on the phone, nauseously chipper at 7:45 AM, was the Ranger's. His pause was a challenge to decode his gibberish and an assumption that I would. An hour or so later, I might have been flattered.

Instead, a late night, a full bladder, an erection and Connie's bare back rising between the duvet and her hair made me not want to play.

A deep breath. "I'm sorry, Mr. Lichtmann, I already gave at the orifice. . ."

"Emanuel, dear boy. I was attending a formal dinner party last night that put me at the same table with Lucius Cohen. As you know, the commissioner and I have certain tastes in common, so our conversation was somewhat intimate. By dessert, we were laughing, ad hilaritatem and well beyond . . . a nice little Oregon pinot that went down like water . . . so I asked him your question."

"Don't torture me, Range', what question was that? The one about the meaning of life?"

"Do you remember asking me to keep my ear to the investigative ground about the matter of the cobweb fracture lines on certain windshields?"

"Yesyesyes, of course, so . . . ?"

"I asked the police commissioner whether they had any leads and he broke out laughing. No, braying would be a better word . . . did you ever notice that he has an accent that only shows up after a bottle and a half of red wine? Well, yes, he is in fact West Indian, from Dominica, and he said the most interesting thing—but excuse me, did I wake you? Am I interrupting something? Perhaps you were changing a verb in one of your insightful reviews from the declarative to the subjunctive mood. I should call back later."

"All right all right, I surrender. What the hell did he say?"

"In essence, he said that if he found the fellow who wielded the BB gun, he would present him with a bottle of champagne and honorary membership in the department. He opined further that any one of his eight thousand officers would grant the fellow permission to sin again. He almost suggested that service revolvers would be offered to the cause."

"Wait, are you telling me that they aren't trying to find out who did it?"

"Not only are they not trying, they are apparently laughing their blue serge asses off. You see, m'boy, the UGA has defended the manufacture of a teflon-coated bullet called the 'cop-killer.' It has the power to penetrate the bullet-proof vests that police officers wear. In fact, slaying the professionally armored officer is this bullet's only purpose. Surprisingly, some of his officers have taken this rather personally: you know how touchy cops can get. Professionally, they restrict themselves to writing up the occasional moving violation and checking the trunk for drug scraps when they see the famous decal, but personally, they seem to be tickled shitless about the shooter. It seems that there's even a rumor that the perp might be a cop. There is no doubt that the commish and his people think of him as a hero."

For a moment, I fought edge-of-the-whirlpool dizziness, for another moment, I gave in.

The Ranger, mistaking my swoon for sleep-benighted incomprehension, went on. "The whole thing has an investigative priority of just below zero, m'boy. It will be investigated right after they figure out who leaves the chewing gum on the seats of the Broad Street bus, but not before. The D.A. doesn't care either, probably wouldn't bother to prosecute unless she was forced to."

"Well, I'm sorry to hear that the mystery won't be solved. Thanks for trying, though. I might just take you out for fugu anyway."

"Doing my best, Emanuel. Pax vobiscum."

A minute later, relieved me, relieved myself, and doubly happy, and so to bed.

30.

April, 2006. Above a concrete palisade there's a six story office building. The windows on the first three stories have been cracked, some of them many times over. At least half are held together with strips of tape. In the center of the facade, above some glass doors that are also cracked, is the polychromed logo of the United Gun Association. The medallion itself is pocked, sandblasted with the indignation of a thousand gas-powered pings.

Inside, there's an office with a gray metal desk set at an angle in the corner near the door. From a seat at the desk, you could read, in reversed out letters on the glass door insert: EXTERNAL COMMUNICATIONS

The light from a cracked and taped window projects a soft spidery pattern on gray industrial carpet. Behind the desk, doodling on a yellow legal pad, is the woman who was in the conference room earlier. She is in shirtsleeves. Her hair, which was once trimmed to just below her ears, is at shoulder length: a softer look. Her desk lamp reflects a yellow glow from the pad into the shadows beneath her chin, lip, nose and eyebrows.

On the wall behind her is a framed card addressed to My Favorite Spokesperson. Next to it is a framed degree, a bachelor's, awarded to Sara Arkwright by the S.I. Newhouse School of Communications in1992.

Sara's proud of her degree. She doodles on her pad, writing in block capitals as she talks on the phone: S.I.N. S.o.C. '92 Then underneath in copperplate cursive: Sin Sucks.

The truth is, Sara thinks to herself, Sin's pretty good business.

"Yeah Mom, I know Mom, it is like working for the Mafia . . . yeah, every time you think they've taken the meanest position they could, they do something worse."

'Mom, listen . . . nobody wants to publish my novel and nobody wants to sweep a thirty-four-year-old ex-field hockey player off her feet and in the meantime, there's the mortgage on the condo. It comes due every month . . . Yeah, I wish you could too Mom . . . Momma dear, I gotta speech that has to be ready in an hour . . . I love you too. Bye."

Sara punches a button on her desk, pauses, breathes in slowly and punches another. "Yes, Sara here. I ordered the surveillance van—it's video equipped, one-way glass, sound recording, the works. Comes with two agents. It'll be in place tomorrow. I worked up a couple of TV talk-show ideas, crime prevention and soft stuff like that. I'll send packages out to our regular contacts by the end of the week. Now on the radio front, I called the regular list, that took all day yesterday, discussed the possibility of their speaking at the convention, told them how much we liked to hear from the stalwart few . . . No, I kept it cheap . . . anyway all of them promised to start talking about it. Oh yeah, I called Grass Roots Inc. They can give us saturation call-in coverage in thirty markets for fifteen hundred per, so I told them to go ahead. Gotta run, gotta meet the press.

In the press room, forty folding chairs, high ceilings with built-in TV lights, small raised stage with a mahogany podium. On the front of the podium is a large version of the United Gun Association logo. Sara walks to the stage from the back of the room, stopping to shake a hand, touch a forearm, wave and smile. About a dozen press people have turned out for this news conference, mostly print, one radio, one CNN. Sara's suit jacket is dark blue with a gray pin stripe, its cut shapes her body into a symbol of the middle ground between dowdy and sexy, leaves her arms free for vigorous, wide-open-spaces salutes to her friends.

A step before reaching the podium, Sara's head pans the room, her face machine-gunning grimaces, winks, eyebrow lifts of personal recognition to the people she missed on the way up. Hours spent in front of the mirror in the Facial Gym pay off.

She ends the series with a look straight into the CNN camera and a squeeze together of the eyebrows. It's the I'm-only-really-here-for-you personal moment before we get down to business. She nails the landing. Seven separate moments of personal contact in less than four seconds. All the Great Ones do it.

"Good Morning and Thank you for coming." The smile has left her lips, lingers for a moment in her eyes and then flickers out.

"As you may have heard, there has been an outbreak of vandalism across the country involving the use of air-powered weapons to break windows that display affiliations with certain groups. This vandalism has been directed against Americans of every political persuasion and represents an attack on our precious First Amendment right to free speech.

"The United Gun Association has stood for the responsible use of firearms since its founding in 1871. The UGA has always been in favor of severe penalties for criminals who misuse firearms. We sympathize with the Americans whose property has been damaged in this epidemic of irresponsibility. This outrage seems to have begun last winter in the Philadelphia area. From there, it has spread like a cancer from Maine to California.

"In keeping with our United Gun Association heritage, we are offering a five-hundred-dollar reward for information leading to the arrest and conviction of anyone using air-powered weapons to vandalize property belonging to members of the United Gun Association. In addition, we are offering a ten-thousand-dollar reward for information leading to the arrest and conviction of anyone who used air-powered weapons to vandalize property belonging to members of the United Gun Association in the Philadelphia area before March of this year.

"Anyone wishing to give information can either fill out the form available at our web site or call toll free. We will respond to everyone who responds to us."

31.

The darkness is relieved with a few soft flashes of light. There's a ponytail of smoke in red then blue. More light dabs, mostly blue, then some pink. It's a bedroom, mounds of covers, Paula's orange cat asleep on one end, Paula coughs again on the other. Daniel enters from the left, naked, carrying a small serving tray.

The light is coming from a luxuriously large color television screen. You could gauge its size from corporal landmarks, nuts-to-nipple height let's say, as Daniel passes in front of it. Daniel and Paula have bought a toy together.

Spoons click in tiny porcelain bowls as they settle in on the view of the screen. The sound is off, Paula and Daniel keeping this luminous thing at a distance. Art not Guest.

On the TV screen, a woman, impossibly tall, starveling. Cheekbones start just below her eyelashes, liquid brown hair stolen from a small woodland mammal. High heeled open toes, loose fitting overalls in some sparklestretchy fabric, nothing else. Taking a few steps, spinning, clutching at the swirling garment, laughing in embarrassment at the peekaboo of garment-baring breast and ribs. Taking, point apparently made, off again. Three steps, another spin, oh my god did that silly fabric slip again and show my hahaha?

Daniel leans back in bed, grabs the remote and hits the POSTERIZE and RANDOM buttons and the model, still mute, turns to silver, her suit persimmon against a background of liverish yellow.

Paula jumps on the jaundiced view. "What's she selling? Quick. Three guesses!"

"Is there a prize?"

"Yes, and there's another one for most creative answer and probably a little something special for Mr. Congeniality."

"All right, I say she's selling breast insurance. No? Teflon soled shoes? That's two . . . umm, I'll tell you, whatever she's selling, I'm buying."

Paula attacks him, throwing a knee over him, rib-tickle fingers burrowing. The covers fall away, she eclipses the soft sun of the set which changes color again: Prussian blue light turns her hair gray, catches the smoke fingers curling, paints her naked back. Blue movie stuff, Paula stays comic. "Bastard!" she giggles, "You're buying what I'm selling and don't you forget it."

Daniel follows the rules of lover wrestling. No offense, defense only. Gasping and giggling, arms and elbows protecting ticklish ribs. "I surrender, mercymercy. I'll give up my horse, the ranch, my gun collection . . . anything."

His words are broken into little gasp-punctuated bundles, the sound absorbed by Paula's torso. Paula stops. The spirit is on her and she is on him.

"Even your gun collection, big boy?"

Paula swings out of the saddle and lies alongside him, the unblocked light washes over them. They squint in the sudden brightness, their bodies carved to monster-movie light and dark by the TV at their feet. The light turns to orange. Can that woman still be doing her idiot dance?

"You know," she says, tracing infinity loops on his chest, "if you gave up your guns, we might just work out something better than 'mercy.' In fact, this could be a whole new approach for me. How many members did you say they have in that UGA? Now if I get naked and tickle two, umm maybe three of them a day. . ."

This time it's Daniel's turn to attack and as the shadow of his body darkens hers and his hands reach her ribs, there's laughter and the slapping of sheets. Her eyes are looking up at him. These eyes are a little wet, a little unhinged, laughing, knowing, wanting.

32.

Hands and coffee cups, oak table. Daniel's cup has a picture of Grover, Paula's has Kermit and Miss Piggy. The parent-in-training cups. The radio is buzzing behind them, pushing its way into their talk.

As Paula stands up to get more coffee, her chair chirps along the floor and they hear the radio host's age-scraped voice ". . . anti-semitism and the other pin-dick afflictions."

"What did he say?" Paula asks.

"Pin dick, pin dick. He said, without saying it, that bigotry is the twin brother of a teeny weeny."

Paula pads toward the kitchen and the radio clicks off. "Wow! if you made an ad campaign out of that . . . I mean, if sex really sells. . ."

"I think that's been established."

"Then no sex or bad sex should be a great un-sell."

"You mean like, 'Vote for Santacci and your genitals will wither'?"

"Or, 'the size of a man's gun collection is inversely proportional to the size of . . . ' "

"I'm not sure you can use the word 'inversely' in an ad."

"Wait, remember that woman on TV last night? The one who was doing all the spinning?"

"No, although I have a very detailed recollection of the woman in front of the TV blocking my view, the one who was doing all the tickling."

"Suppose what she was saying was, 'if you do guns, you won't do me,' or 'pick your bang-bang brother, if you wanna have one, you can't have the other.' "

"In fact, a certain beautiful woman said something very much like that to me—something about showing me a real good time if I just gave her my gun collection."

Paula turns off the radio with a snap and takes the one cassette tape from her collection that's migrated to Daniel's. It's his favorite, he says,

Paula with her mom belting out show tunes. The best part, he swears, is when they do selections from "Annie, Get Your Gun."

33.

In a parking lot near the Philadelphia waterfront, two nuns—one tall, sturdy and young, the other gray and petite—are standing in front of a cinderblock one-story building. The sun is low-angled and bright, and the wind sticks their dark blue overcoats to their right sides. It's hold-on-to-your-wimple weather. The letters wrapped around the building say WAL-MART

An identically dressed nun comes out of the building, smiles, nods, and slips a small spiral-bound notebook into her coat pocket. The three nuns go through the automatic doors and back into the store. One of the nuns may have said "thank you" as the door opened for her.

They take a shopping cart. The nuns don't take off their black coats which, incidentally, seem to be all the same size, but their habits are blue, below-the-knee dresses. Their headgear announces their status without concealing much hair, and their voices are lost in the store babel and in the rattle of the cart.

The tall one on the right curves her shoulders forward in a stoop and walks with a checked step, as if she trained to match her stride to other, shorter people. The fingers of her left hand are barely touching the handle of the cart.

On the left, medium height, broad-shouldered and striding, is the sister of our stereotypes. Her head pans the aisles, her left hand waves to the children, her right hand is guiding the shopping cart. Her body jerks away from the group. She wants to stop and chat up that mother with the two toddlers, but the force of some gravity pulls her back. In profile she is strong-jawed and pale as she swivels to smile bye-bye.

The shortest, oldest one is in the middle. She walks a step behind the other two who occasionally turn to her and point to something, explaining this or that. She is included, protected, not left behind.

In hardware, they pick out a cable cutter and hang it over the edge of the cart, one handle in, the other out. There is no discussion of options, no sisterly consensus making. They know their cable cutters. The nuns are suddenly less casual, focused more on the things ahead of them, less on the people around them.

At house wares they turn right. In the second aisle, two sixteen-gallon kitchen trash cans, the kind with the swinging tops that protect you from having to look at your garbage, go into the cart, side by side. One more aisle, another left between the walls of cleaning products, they stop in front of a display of Alkazolve!tm The Super Strength Drain Cleaner for Plastic Pipes. The sociable sister reads the label of the 48 oz. yellow plastic bottle, directing her words at the short one: "It says right here, Sister Marguerite, that Alkazolve! should never be used on metal pipes since it is corrosive and can cause instant and irreparable damage to metal surfaces."

"Then we'll have to be very careful, Sister Kate," Sister Marguerite replies, nodding her head in an exaggerated way that suggests that they are exchanging ritual reassurance, not information.

"You be careful too, Carmella dear," she adds, naming the tall one for us.

Then Marguerite pulls rubber gloves from her coat pocket. In a second, the three nuns are opening bottles of Alkazolve! and pouring them in the trash cans. They open more than a dozen bottles, taking their time and pouring carefully. One bottle with its cap loosely replaced, goes in the cart with the garbage cans.

The empty bottles placed neatly on the floor, Sister Marguerite wriggles her way around the other two, past the cart. The camera follows her as she makes a right at the end of the cleaning products aisle, goes three aisles over, turns left, walks another aisle's length and stops.

She is standing in sporting goods, looking straight ahead at the gun department. There is a counter with boxes of ammunition and a selection of pistols. Access to the salesmen's area is through a waist-high gate with a heavy lock. On the wall behind the counter is a display of long guns in a glass-fronted case.

"Young man, could you help me?" Sister is talking to a pale young man with black hair and a sparse black mustache. He is reading a magazine whose cover looks to her like an indecipherable maze of runic neon. He puts down his magazine and walks to the locked gate, his face set in the mask called Benevolence to the Clergy.

As he opens the gate, two things happen at once.

Sister Marguerite turns away from the youngster, leading him to a display of lanterns a few steps away. As she does, the two other sisters arrive, the tall one pushing the cart, Sister Kate in front.

Kate grabs the gate as it closes and holds it open as Carmella pushes the cart through and into the protected rectangle of gun space. As the clerk turns to follow them, the gate clicks shut and Sister Marguerite bumps him and lifts his key ring which had been hanging on a hook from his belt.

"Hey, sister, you can't go back there!" he says to the two nuns who are already undeniably back there.

"Oh son, don't worry, they mean no harm, no harm at all," Sister Marguerite insists, spinning him back to her with her words as she hands the keys across the counter to Sister Kate.

The boy is trapped outside as surely as the nuns are locked inside. Marguerite has him engaged, her blue eyes synchromeshed to his brown. He can't turn away from a chatty nun. The other two sisters do not even lift their eyes to him.

"Ammo case is that little red-tagged brass one," Carmella says, indicating the key to the bullet chest. Kate opens the lock to the ammunition counter and hands the key ring to Carmella who finds the key she needs without fumbling. She opens the two locks on the long-gun case and grabs the cable cutters with an easy, almost practiced gesture. She cuts the security cables that hold the long guns in place through their trigger guards.

Sister Marguerite's eyes flicker to his name tag.

"So tell me . . . Anthony . . . where are you from?"

Anthony and Marguerite's voices fade out, their faces become blurs in the foreground. In sharp focus between them, we see Kate and Carmella opening boxes of ammunition and dumping them into the garbage cans filled with solvent.

Back to Anthony. Marguerite is saying something interrogative about brothers and sisters and Anthony pulls back from her and runs through the growing crowd of shoppers and carts to the front of the store.

"Well, I held him as long as I could. He seemed like such a nice boy. How's it going?"

"We're almost done with the bullets, but these fumes are awful." Kate's nose is wrinkled, her eyes squinting.

We see Carmella dropping two pistols, holsters and all, into her can. We see her turn to the upright case and set the guns two at a time, stock down, in a garbage can. Careful, no splashing. It's a few minutes of smelly work until they hear a man's voice saying, "Step aside please, police officers."

We see Carmella's face, long and intense. She frowns. Will she have time? She opens the reserve bottle of drain cleaner just as two uniformed police officers appear in the space in front of the counter.

"Michael Joseph Luzzi! We heard that this was your shift. How nice to see you."

The officer sweeps the gun department with his eyes. It looks like a clear-cut case of vandalism in progress. In another minute, everything in the WAL-MART gun department will be destroyed. It's time for action.

Officer Luzzi takes a deep breath. "Sister Marguerite," he says, "I wonder if you've met my partner, Officer Durand? Kateesha, this is Sister Marguerite Ahearn."

"So very nice to meet you, dear, it's just like Michael Joseph to team up with the prettiest girl around."

Kateesha, who must be used to being called pretty, is trying very hard not to laugh. Her eyes flick uncertainly toward the nuns behind the counter and back to her partner. She looks as if she's already figuring out the different ways that she's going to tell this story.

Sister Carmella is pouring the extra Alkazolve! over the long guns. Her head is tilted back and away from the can, her eyes shut. "We're done Sister," she says.

"Thank you, Sister, come out from there, you too Sister Kate." Turning to the policemen, "You know Michael, we were doing this for you . . . but I suppose you'll have to arrest us now, won't you dear?"

"Well, I don't know, Sister . . . I guess we'll have to arrest those two sisters over there." The younger nuns smile crookedly at him and raise their eyes. Sister Kate seems to be sprouting a tear. The arrest was built into the decision to do this, they are exalted, not afraid. "But I didn't see you doing anything."

Kate and Carmella peel off their gloves and leave them on the counter. Their hands go in skirt pockets and come out holding ferocious single-action rosary beads. Magnums.

"Well, you should probably arrest me anyway, dear . . . conspiracy or something like that."

To the crowd that's gathered, Sister Marguerite raises her hand in the gesture of blessing. She raises her voice, speaks to the people in the crowd.

"You see, we can fight back. Let's not be afraid of guns anymore, let's make the guns be afraid of us. Pray for us and these officers too. We shall overcome. God bless you all. Come along, Sisters, these officers are very busy."

Sister Marguerite and officer Luzzi walk slowly to the front of the store. He is silently forgiving her for an injustice she perpetrated on him in fourth grade. A few steps behind them, Sister Kate and Carmella are flanking Officer Durand. Children who were somnambulant with fascination a few minutes before are being pushed toward the nuns whose hands are reaching out to them. Heads are being touched, not ruffled. It's a blessing. The spirit moves and the five blue uniforms seem to merge into a single arrowhead block that moves up and away. Children push their way into the aisle as the block gets bluer and blurrier, smaller and, for all they know, closer to heaven.

Sister Marguerite's voice is saying ". . . and your sister Veronica, is she still with the Inquirer?"

From the back of the store, in guns and sporting goods, a raggedy, scratching sound rises. It might be applause.

34.

Inside Odetta: Cardoso is dining alone, dawdling with an appetizer of black rice timbale and saffron crusted sashimi, keeping thoughtful communion with a decanter of red wine. Over the light clatter of the room, he motions for Paula.

Cardoso is whispering. "I thought you might like to know that a detective agency from Washington has applied for a permit to do some work here. They'll be setting up a surveillance van, brown and gold, Delaware plates, with video cameras to capture the image of anyone attempting to vandalize it. Inside are two college track athletes to catch the vandal and wrestle her to the ground. They plan to stay as long as they need to."

Paula notices the feminine pronoun, not usually used as a vicar for 'vandal.' She remains waitress cool. "Yes?" she says as if waiting for the punch line.

"The most interesting feature of the van is a decal on the back. One that says United Gun Association." Cardoso looks away, changes the subject. "My companion should be here any minute, would you mind bringing another dinner menu?"

Paula's vision goes blurry, she whirls with hypoxia as she forgets to breathe, feels the rush of air from her lungs as she realizes that this man could, but hasn't, hurt her.

"Sure," she says and wonders if she chirped the word out or if it squeaked and popped up from the floor like a cartoon mouse.

When Paula returns with the menu, Lichtmann is seated across from Cardoso. Their faces dance a little ballet of inquiry, assurance, commencement. As Paula hands Lichtmann his menu, he touches her hand.

"Good shooting the other night, my dear. But for that fellow jumping out at you, I would have awarded you both ears and the antenna." His voice is soft, confidential. Of course, the little man with the cane, the one Daniel told her about. "What's that little ziggurat you're attack-ing, Emanuel?" He too relieves her of the burden of reply.

Paula thinks. She would love to attack that van on purpose, walk into their trap and win. She hears Daniel's voice saying "the real power isn't in popping windshields" and it doesn't matter. Paula's a shooter now. There's a feeling that she gets and that's the feeling she wants.

In the staff bathroom, Paula takes a tiny red phone from her purse, calls Daniel.

"Hi, I'll be a little bit late tonight."

"Sorry to hear that, I rented a copy of 'Coconuts' and picked up a quart of Rocky Road. What's up?"

"Nothing. Just something I have to do."

"Going skating?"

"Don't worry, I won't be long."

And Daniel, having nothing else to say, says, "Be careful."

Paula makes a kissing sound and hangs up.

Paula's apartment smells empty, stale. The cat spent last weekend at Daniel's and there are no litter and kibble smells. In a whiff or two, this has become a place where she gets her mail, changes her clothes. She looks at the cabinet full of tapes, her life in music, and she wishes she had the time to play something. It seems colder in the living room than she remembers it and she doesn't dare to open the refrigerator.

She sockpads her way down the steps, straps on skates and push-es off along the sidewalk. If Tom hadn't died, no, if they hadn't killed Tom, she thinks, she would be spending tonight at Skipper's with her old gang. When did they become the "old," she wonders. Do you just skate away from things like that?

In only a few minutes, she's warmed up, taken her sweatshirt off and tied it around her waist. Her strides are long and powerful and she jumps over the humps in the root-wrinkled concrete.

There's a van with Delaware plates, but it's painted white with three Chinese ideographs on the side. Another van—what color is brown under pink street lights anyway? Then she sees it, two parking tickets under its wiper blade, dull brown, two-tone, nondescript.

Paula skates past in black spandex, checking the decal. At the corner she fiddles with her bag, pulls something out, ducks her head, turns and heads back. A few slow strokes to steady her hand, she brakes at the van's window and brings her bag to point blank range. She squeezes the trigger, her face inches away from the glass and the video camera. The side doors blow open, two husky youths in sweats and sneakers spring to the curb, martial arts movie moves. She drops down and powers off, arms swinging. The boys accelerate magnificently, a hand brushes her sweat shirt. She pulls away from them, a two-yard gap with a few strokes of her blades. They run, arms pumping, Paula looks over her shoulder, loses a yard.

They follow from behind, excited by the chase, eyes on her ass. They follow up Fifteenth to Spruce Street, left on Spruce, strong arms five or six feet behind her. One of the boys lunges as she turns, trying for a tackle, missing and bouncing his face one, two, slide, the stones in the concrete sidewalk like teeth in the pink street light.

As she turns on Spruce, she sees a fault line in the paving squares a few yards ahead. Slightly off balance, she bends her knees and springs over it. She comes down on one skate, whips her arms to get upright again and the maneuver almost stops her. She hits a stretch of brick cross-laid sidewalk and feels the vibrations up to her ears just as she feels a hand grab her hip. The hand slips, then grazes her left shoulder and she can hear the man breathing as she lurches to the right and stumbles against a parked car.

The force of his lunge and her sudden stop send him past her and into the railing at the edge of a stoop. The sweatshirt comes off her waist and he holds it out in front of him as he crashes into the wrought iron.

Paula walks her way off the curb and into the street. She grabs the latch handle of a truck pulling out with a change of light. She takes the truck as far as Seventeenth and swings left against the traffic for half a block. She slows down at a garbage can, squats to check her reflection in the basement window of a row house. She's looking into the smiling face of Mickey Mouse. Paula lifts the Mask and places it gently on top of the pile in the can. She is gasping, gulping down air. Her stride is heavy and short as she pushes her way west, looking over her shoulder and wondering about a long route home.

35.

Paula and Daniel are sitting at poles of his round oak table. The fruited plane is between them. Paula has raided it for a tiny bunch of grapes sitting on a paper napkin in front of her. One of the bright brass C-shaped candlesticks is at Daniel's left hand, the other is at Paula's right.

Daniel. The wrinkled toe of a black wing-tipped shoe tapping the meter of emphasis as he speaks. Sing what I say. Soft pants, lightly swollen, the plaid that dare not speak its name. Pale tan shirt, coarse-woven wool tie, sleeves rolled up, prepared to work. Rough and ready. Enlarged at the groin, feet on the ground, toes could fly away on black angel wings.

He speaks: "We're at a crisis here so some things may get rushed, born before their time." He looks away for a second. "Did I tell you that when I started putting on weight, my Dad called it premature girth?"

"But anyway." They are looking at each other in a perfect stillness. Daniel drops his eyes, looking far out to C and away from Paula. She will have some privacy in the middle of this invasion.

"I love you and I want to protect you and I want you to have what you want . . . I'm . . . uh, I'm a little confused about my role here, but why should that stop me?"

Paula frisks him with her eyes. Here's a man who hides his best, puts his presents behind the tree.

Daniel says "I'm worried for you, sweetheart. You've had two close brushes with being caught, now there's a reward . . . I promised you that I'd never let my own shit about being straight up get in the way of what you had to do, but now I'm scared for you. I don't want to tell you what you should do, I just want to know that you understand the danger you're in. I guess I want you to know that your danger is mine now."

"I love your being 'straight up.' It's one of the nicest things about you." Paula smiles at her little dirty joke, Daniel smiles back.

He moves to her end of the table, dragging his chair with him. He takes her hand. "I couldn't stand anything hurting you," Daniel says. There is another silence between them. This isn't strategy talk between old friends, this is cutting edge intimacy talk: new lovers: here honey, have a grape. They hear the silence out. It's a question, a proposal, a "shall we dance?" a "bite this apple, buster?"

"Yes," Paula says, accepting his hypothesis that they're in it together, raising him one by acting as if she assumed it all along and has held his feelings next to her heart the whole time. "When I started fighting back, it really freed me. Now it seems childish . . . and scary too. I'm not afraid of being caught by the police, it's the anger of all these gun freaks and what they might do to us."

The "us" echoes. Daniel's brain vibrates with it in two-tenth second strobe between black and white, the new pronoun taking its place at his, no, "their" table. He would cry, hug her, slay the fatted tofu and make sacrifice. He will butter the bread of her risky declaration by making believe he knew it all along.

"You know people's cars are very personal. You can attack their right to blow up Bambi and they'll probably want to debate, but when you attack their cars it's like hitting them. I worry about what they could do to us too. I want you to stop shooting."

"I know, I have to stop doing this."

"You know all you have to do to stop is . . . well, just stop. I don't think it's habit-forming and no one knows it's you. You could just stop and be safe."

"It makes me sad to think about it."

"About what?"

"About stopping fighting . . . about letting them go on doing this to us . . . about Tom. "

"But you started something, I mean look at what's going on all over the country. "

"I guess I mean I'd miss being a part of it . . . no, I'd miss the rush it gives me too. I like the way I feel these days, I don't want to give it up."

"Well, I've got a secret for you. I know you like the feeling you get when you're out hunting. I can tell by the way you act when you come back. I know from the way you are in bed." Paula starts to speak, but can't make an honest sound. Daniel continues, "Suppose I told you that I knew something even better."

Daniel gets up, walks behind her. His hands rest on her shoulders. "There's another way and I think you're going to love it, people think it's even sexier than pellet pistols. I have some ideas . . . they're not all thought out, but maybe . . ."

She takes his hand, moves him to the couch, and an hour or so later, there's a plan.

Later on in bed, Paula's face is pinched in concentration, her finger punching out the ideas in the air, Daniel smiling, nodding, midwifing the thoughts. Their room is filled with music—that saxophone solo from the Rolling Stones' "Waiting on a Lady." On a night table a framed photo of Paula and Tom. His arm is around her shoulder and she is smiling.

A WORKBOOK IN POLITICAL IMAGING

From Chapter 4 SLOGANIZATION OF THE AMBIENT IDEOLOGY . . . ultimate useful reduction of a complex idea is its expression as a geometric shape or solid color.

*For much of the last century, there was a political movement called Marxism that appropriated the color red to stand for a set of ideas that were both complex and speculative.

From Chapter 6 IMAGINOGENESIS . . . it is necessary that the sloganized icon be associated with a set of images that test out as

* exciting
* affiliative
* reassuring

36.

Paula is standing by the two oak shelves in Daniel's dining room, just to the left of the fruited plane. In the foreground are two soiled place settings, some used groceries, a pad and pencil and Daniel. He is sitting behind one of the plates, carefully arranging a ragtag mob of rigatoni into a well-drilled regiment. Paula is tapping a number into a telephone.

A phone rings on a wooden desktop a few blocks away. Oak again, Arts and Crafts. The desk is breathlessly neat: a Macintosh computer screen as thin and as sharp as a sail is wrapped in a clear plastic dust shield. Four sharpened pencils are arrayed as neatly as Daniel's rigatoni next to a perfectly squared up eye-ease green steno notebook. The hand that grabs the phone is Cardoso's.

"Hi, this is Paula . . . from Odetta?"

"Of course, hi Paula, how are you?"

"I'm fine, just fine . . . I need to talk to you about . . . about what you told me the other night when you and your friend were in for dinner."

"Well, a word to the wise is . . . a cliché."

"You knew it was me."

"Of course. No, I mean yes. Yes, I knew. I saw you one night back in February, on Seventeenth Street A few minutes after you shot, I walked past the car, saw what you were up to. It intrigued me, this thing that you were doing. I asked a friend to, uh, find out if the police were investigating the broken windshield thing. He saw you too, the other night when you whacked that car in front of the Forrest Theater. You've seen him with me in Odetta too, he's that short, well-dressed fellow. He was the one who tripped the guy who was chasing you on Walnut Street, the one that made sure your boyfriend got a ride home from the white and blue taxi company."

"Oh." Paula sees the rest of the story, connects with her local fan club. Windshield whacking, she figures, was a spectator sport all along.

She's the star player—boys love sports. This should be easy. "I'd like to talk to you . . . in person, I mean."

"Well, sure, umm—" Cardoso pantomimes looking quickly left right, searching for exits. In the dining room, Daniel gets up from the table, stacks both plates on one hand, takes glasses in another and leaves for the kitchen.

"Do you have a minute now?" Paula is pinched tight, shallowbreathing and nervous.

Cardoso's apartment. The sound of scuffly steps outside and a knock, tentative, then another, firmer, take charge assertive what-kind-of-man-am-I knock. It's Paula, wearing her waitress suit. Her eyes are wide open and set, firmly looking ahead at something Cardoso doesn't see.

Cardoso has given this encounter a few minutes of thought. He leads Paula down a hall past two closed doors to his kitchen, to a small drop-leafed table that abuts a wall underneath a pass-through opening. He has changed clothes. When she called, he was wearing a t-shirt; now he's wearing a white turtleneck with an old black cardigan over it. "Do you take it black?"

This, pointing to an old-fashioned espresso machine.

"Yes, just sugar, no lemon peel thanks."

Cardoso smiles as if he'd just been offered the secret handshake and busies himself with cups and levers and whooshes of steam that sound like protracted blasts of Paula's air pistol.

Paula scans the apartment, her look is bemused, she is enjoying some secret joke. Cardoso's apartment is a lot like Daniel's, eccentric and comfortable and supernaturally neat. She notices the oak table, the sensuously stuffed couch, the wonder of the fat armchair whose back legs have been sawn off so that it tilts up like a hungry-mouthed hopper.

Paula sits. "My boyfriend's desk looks just like that except yours is even neater."

For eight-tenths of a second, Cardoso's face morphs into Daniel's, stops about halfway, returns. Paula shakes it off, gulps big air. Cardoso mistakes her anxiety. He says, "I want you to know that I'm not going to turn you in . . . what you're doing means a lot to me."

Paula blinks at the sudden change in reality. "You don't want the reward?"

"No. There isn't anything I could buy with it . . . nothing that would make up for what I would lose. Listen, you should know, or . . . no, I have to tell you that I've been watching you come back from your hunting trips since last winter. I watch you from the window." He tilts his head in the direction of the living room, "or from up on the roof." He points his eyebrows.

"I don't want to do true confessions here, but I was feeling kind of dazed and numb the first night I saw you go shooting. Somehow, watching you changed all that. I guess that makes me sort of a Peeping Tom."

Paula freezes as Cardoso's "Tom" seems to echo.

Cardoso continues, "But I guess you've inspired a lot of other people too. Did you hear about those nuns who took out the gun department at the South Philly Wal-Mart?"

Paula is unfrozen but not moving, her coffee cup just below lip level. She, almost a light source in the windowless kitchen, is looking at him, barely smiling, fully there. Paula has lit on a branch, doesn't know which one. The woman is strong enough to make him wait and she does. And then:

"Thank you. Thank you . . . this is a whole lot easier than I thought it was going to be. I want to ask you a favor. It's a big favor."

"I owe you one."

"I want you to turn me in and collect the reward. Wait . . . there's more. I want you—no, I need you to promise me that you won't tell anyone that I asked you to do it."

Daniel is at home alone. He is sitting on the couch where we saw him last stroking Paula. Daniel is watching his own movie. It ends with him losing Paula, and it stars Manny Cardoso. He is rehearsing the feeling, assuring himself that he will be all right no matter what. He is hugging himself. Not craven or desolate, it's a pass-the-time-in-courage embrace.

We hear the sound of locks, thunks of bolts, clanging applause of keys. Paula lets herself in.

Daniel turns to her, loosening his grip, and she says, "He had to think it over."

"You mean ten grand didn't—?"

"No, it didn't. I think he has all the money he wants."

Daniel sags a little, Paula straightens, strips off her coat. He hugs her with surprising force, burying his face in her hair. Sniffing, perhaps for infidelity.

The phone rings.

Cardoso on the right, engulfed in his cut-back reclining hopper chair. There is a gray and white striped cat lying across the low point of his lap, facing us, her head just higher than the arm of the chair. Cardoso's eyes are closed and he is speaking slowly, building a monologue to stand on.

"I understand. I mean I understand what you want and I think I understand why you want it. I don't think I could turn you in and make believe that I was being a good citizen, bringing a criminal to justice. I'm not strong enough to be your Judas, not that good an actor either. I'm sorry."

Click.

"He won't do it."

"It's time for Plan B." Daniel's voice is not exactly smug, but we can hear the swelling of a light relief.

"What's Plan B?" Paula is puzzled. Was there a piece of this that she forgot?

"We don't have one."

Paula laughs, remembers why she's falling in love with this man. "The Scalp Hunters is on at nine."

"Good, I picked up some Rum Raisin."

As Paula's half-weary, raised eyebrow smile is just forming, the phone rings again. It's Cardoso.

"I've changed my mind. I'll turn you in, just as you asked. I'll write a piece for the Forum and I'll try to get them to run it front page. I'll keep quiet about my intentions for a month, thirty days. The media will eat this up, you give them a good story and they'll do your work for you.

"The second I get the check, I will endorse it over to Handgun Control or Cease Fire or one of those . . . but I'll ask them not to make it public. I will have to tell one person and that's my friend Connie. I think you know who she is . . . you've seen us together in Odetta."

Paula looks at Daniel, her shoulders start forward, her lips start to open with a report, a question. And then she stops.

"Manny, you'll do what you need to do, but I have to ask you not to tell her. For at least a month. I need that time. If you tell even one person, it could keep me from doing what I have to do. I'll do anything you want, but I need you to wait. Can you promise me that?"

An article in the Forum, front page, above the fold
WINDOW SMASHING VIGILANTE UNMASKED!

Sometime last winter, when the cold had slowed, if not closed down, the street crime action, Philadelphia's urban imagination was captured by a new kind of bandit. This desperado roamed the city's streets at night, using a BB gun to shoot out the windows of cars that displayed the sticker of the United Gun Association.

Somehow, this one individual with a bundle of BBs broke the dam that held back an American reservoir of resentment against guns. Within weeks of this crime spree being reported in these pages, the idea caught on across the country. The Auto Insurance Institute estimates that insurance claims for windshield vandalism increased nationwide by 2700%.

There may have been insufficient windshields to go around. Incidents of crime directed at gun owners became more and more frequent, and more imaginative. Consider:

* In California, a trailer load of the inexpensive pistols called Saturday Night Specials was hijacked by a team of masked and scantily clad women and driven into the ocean on a beach near Leucadia. The hijackers left a note apologizing for "any environmental damage we may have caused."

* The fire alarm system was triggered at a gun factory in Springfield, Massachusetts causing an estimated $800,000 worth of damage to a production run of easily concealable .38 caliber pistols. The building was empty except for a janitorial crew. Within a week, similar "accidents" had been reported at arms factories in Exeter, New Hampshire, West Hurley, New York, Genesco, Illinois and Grand Island, Nebraska.

*A trio of nuns from the St. Martin De Porres Elementary School in South Philadelphia were arrested for destroying guns and ammunition in a discount store display. A diocesan spokesman said: "While we can never rejoice when someone breaks the law, actions that seem criminal in the short run may sometimes prove to be Godly in the long run."

As the crimes multiplied, the gun manufacturers and the United Gun Association kept silent. Apparently they were concerned that publicity would only fuel more incidents. Early this spring, however, they realized that they had a serious problem on their hands. A lobby that owns a dozen senators and scores of congressional representatives was being laughed at on late night TV. Even their right-wing allies were deserting them as "too soft" to defend themselves.

"How many UGA members does it take to screw in a lightbulb?
Three.
One to screw in the bulb and two to put a bullet proof vest on it."

Worst of all for the gun lobby, police across the nation were reacting with massive indifference to this crime wave. In some cities there were even rumors that the perpetrators might themselves be policemen.

Last week, the UGA decided to act. At a low-key press conference, UGA spokesman Sara Arkwright announced a reward.

Well, this columnist is claiming it. I know that at least one early incident was the work of a single person, not a gang. I saw that person at work.

Late one night in February, I watched as a woman in a black trench coat walked past a Jeep Wagoneer parked on 17th Street between Pine and Delancey. I had had dinner earlier at Spencer's. I was remembering the exquisite ballotine of chicken with shiitake stuffing and thinking about the adorable student waitress with her thumb in my *gallette des pommes.* I was wondering if the sauce for the ballotine had been made from a pure chicken stock or if a few roasted veal bones had crept in. But I digress.

I saw the woman on Seventeenth Street look at something on the rear windshield of the car, turn around and put her hand in the brown shoulder bag that she wore, in city-safe fashion, across her chest. I heard a whooshing sound and a crack and then the woman walked on south to Pine Street and turned left.

A few minutes later, I walked over to the car and saw that the rear windshield was sporting a United Gun Association decal and was cracked. The crack centered on the decal.

Furthermore, I recognized the vandal. She is my neighbor, Paula Sherman, a waitress at Odetta on Seventeenth St. She was the victim last fall of a street assault with a pistol in which her companion was shot to death and her image and words were appropriated by a certain politician seeking re-nomination.

I hereby claim the $10,000 reward from the UGA. I've faxed them a copy of this article. Watch this space for further developments.

37.

Daniel in blue blazer and tie is peering through the clutter of a television studio. He has read the Workbook in Political Imaging and he's ready to test market some symbols. Vignetted by cables, lights and booms is a large yellow-feathered creature, lumpy, roughly pear shaped. Its wings are vestigial, arm-like and its hands are unctuously clasped together.

Big Bird keeps her hands together as she faces a crowd of two dozen six-year-olds. "Hi everybody. Today we're going to sing a kind of song called a round. To sing a round we need to break up into groups. Won't that be fun? I have some buttons here and I'm going to spread them out on the floor. Now just come on over and take a button. Then everybody who has the same color button will be in a group together."

Daniel is suddenly intent on a spread of buttons with blue, green and red circles printed on them. Little hands are picking up buttons, putting some back, grabbing for others. In a few seconds, all the blue ones are gone, then the green and finally, grudgingly, like the runt puppy at the pound, the red ones are taken.

A little girl cries because she didn't get a blue circle, a boy hands her his, she smiles at him. Big Bird dips her head to pat the boy, her tail bounces, throwing a plume of dust into the light. She swings around to stage right, head up, signaling to somebody. One purple lid comes down over a ping-pong ball eye, the two lower fingers on her hands fold to the palm. A wink and a thumbs-up.

Follow her gaze, it's Daniel in the shade of an enormous light stand, mouthing the word 'blue,' returning the thumbs-up, smiling.

Cardoso's Diary 7
······································

Until recently, I had noticed other people's feelings about me in the same way that a trout notices rain. Esteem or distaste might eventually trickle down to me in some way, but they never had any direct impact. I attended them without emotion. I was curious or cautious, but never touched.

So while I was not surprised that my fingering Paula had made me the neighborhood creep, I was shocked at how much it hurt. My usual cruise through the 'hood, supermarket, fish store and greengrocers, has turned into a volley of averted eyes and barely muffled comments.

Except for Connie . . . I can't understand Connie. Women have left me all my life for reasons that I would listen to but never understand, and this one is staying for reasons that I can't even imagine.

Last night I asked her why and she said, "Well, I know something about you and that something makes me want to fuck your brains out and then keep you with me for the rest of my life."

I hugged her, buried my face in her belly. "Wait a minute," she said," you're all right with that? This is where I usually lose 'em . . . oh, migod, I have to tell you. . ." And then I was kissing her and what she had to tell me had to wait.

PEACE ON THE STREETS CAMPAIGN
565 S. 16th Street Philadelphia, PA 19146
www.peacestreets.org

Roselle Cutner, Chair
The Hon. Carter Davidson
Luther Stokes Ferguson
The Rev. Telly Henderson
Ch. Inspector Angel Ramirez
Paula Sherman
Irenia Jones-Thomas
Claris Yale

Dear Friend,

Thank you for your inquiry. We're enclosing a sample of our poster blank. Follow the instructions on the blank itself. You can then reproduce as many copies as you can use. The quick-print shop that does your printing can probably supply you with paste and brushes.

If you have any questions, or need help getting your poster ready, please drop by our office at Bethany Baptist Church, or look up our web site.

Peace,
Roselle Cutner

38.

Inside a warehouse, the lights are acid etching a young man in a pale suit. He holds a microphone and is bouncing lightly on his toes, waiting to speak. His hair is piled in an amber wave. He is smiling broadly, his teeth perfect cue balls of brightness. Staring into them, you could see the future. The camera's red light has released him from the bottle of silence and he begins.

"The newest development in the Paula Sherman case is the curious lack of developments. Sherman, a Center City resident, is the principal suspect in an incident involving shooting at the window of an empty car with a BB gun. It was an act of vandalism that many people feel was the beginning of the current wave of actions against gun owners and gun merchants that is sweeping the country.

"In the days since Sherman was identified by an informant, the Philadelphia District Attorney's Office has made no move to prosecute Sherman for the crime."

The screen frames a black-suited cherubic androgyne, aging and adorable. She is standing behind a haystack of letters that is almost a foot tall.

"We're here with Philadelphia District Attorney, Nancy Ryan. Can you tell us what those letters are?"

"These are letters urging us to move more quickly and to prosecute severely in the Paula Sherman case. Many of them are coupon letters, torn from magazines. The ones that are actually written have pretty much the same words as the coupons. This is junk mail in reverse, part of an orchestrated campaign by the gun groups."

"So you haven't been persuaded by them to bring charges against Ms. Sherman?"

"No, the District Attorney's office has its hands full with the crime load created by real guns, and all we have here frankly, is an alleged eyewitness who happens to write for a weekly newspaper . . . A broken window doesn't get the same attention that an armed robbery does. We still have to investigate the case. A mail-in campaign doesn't change our priorities. We have paid a lot more attention to these letters, though." She moves to her right, the camera follows, and on the other end of the table we see another pile of letters, twice the height, eight times the volume. "These are letters from people urging us not to prosecute. Some of them are urging us to work for tougher gun laws, and there is a different kind of pile I'd like to show you."

She turns away and we follow around a partition to a locked door in a heavy wire cage. Our guide says a cheery hello, the door opens and we follow her, wondering. On the floor in front of us and next to some heavy metal shelving with labeled boxes is a pile of guns, mostly pistols, mostly small. There are a few weapons that we've seen before on news footage from remote mountainous regions, dull gray things with slings and curved clips.

"These are guns that have been turned in to various city agencies this year. Most of them have come in the days since Ms Sherman came to our attention and almost all of them were unregistered."

"Thank you, Ms Ryan."

The camera moves in on the man in the light suit. "Meanwhile, in Harrisburg, angry members of the State Legislature are demanding that the state police take immediate action and arrest Paula Sherman. Back to you, Ann."

FAXFAXFAXFAXFAXFAXFAXFAXFAXFAX
FAXFAXFAXFAXFAXFAX

WASHINGTONIAN PHARMACY PUBLIC FAX !!

A BUCK A PAGE!!

FAXFAXFAXFAXFAXFAXFAXFAXFAXFAXFAX

FAXFAXFAXFAXFAX

TO: Peace on the Streets Campaign

FR: A friend

The next few pages of this fax are a memorandum of agreement between the United Gun Association and a company called Grass Roots, Inc. It calls for Grass Roots to conduct a saturation campaign of radio call-in shows in thirty markets including Philadelphia. In each city, people will be paid to call radio shows and express their outrage about the wave of vandalism directed at UGA members. As you'll see, the UGA pays $1,500 to buy this support in each city.

A copy of this memo is also being sent to the Philadelphia Forum Newspaper. I hope you can put it to good use. Good luck.

A friend

39.

Outside, on a broad, brick-paved plaza edged with flowering cherry trees. The building in the background is the Constitution Center. Small gray clouds mottle the sky and the wind is gusting, flogging the long line of people who are waiting for admission to the center.

The set of low deep steps in the foreground seems made for performances of high school glee clubs. Paula is standing at the top of those steps. Daniel is with her, just behind and to her left. There are a dozen reporters, a handful of sound technicians fiddling with cables. There's the Newslady. She is modestly put together, trench coated and sneakered. Her hair is held in place against the wind by a scarf tied and tucked headband style. There are a few other locally well-known haircuts and a youngish reporter from CNN. Distributed around the edges of the crowd are four large people in black leather jackets. The jackets have the words CEASE FIRE painted on the back in white. The American flag on the steeple of the Center is blown almost flat.

Paula taps one of the microphones in front of her and smiles. Her hair, blown sideways, has the dignity and vulnerability of a tattered flag. Her freckles are invisible, her skin is pale and radiant, professionally done, no-make-up look.

"Good morning. I hope none of you are being blown away—at least not yet. I want to thank you all for coming out this morning. I know that Mr. Farber promised you a significant break in the story of America's Rebellion Against Gun Deaths." Another small smile and Paula leans forward confidentially. "I don't think you'll be disappointed."

"Last fall, a dear friend of mine was murdered on a city street as he and I walked home from work. He was killed because a criminal was able to get his hands on a pistol and use it in an attempted robbery. For reasons that we don't know, in the course of that robbery, my friend was shot to death.

"I say that we don't know why my friend Tom died that night and in a sense that's true . . . we'll never know. But in another sense, the reason that this sweet, caring young man is dead is all too painfully obvious. He is dead because the robber had easy access to a weapon that could kill from a distance. Without that gun, my friend might have been hurt, or frightened, but he would definitely be alive today.

"Now I don't expect any of you to be shocked by this story. There's no reason why you should be. A person being shot to death is a pretty common occurrence. In the two hundred days since Tom died, one hundred and eighty-eight people in Philadelphia have died from gun shots. They ranged in age from six years old to seventy-four. How could you be shocked at a thing that happens almost once a day? It's really business as usual here in Philadelphia and all across America. Ninety people a day. Bang, bang, bang.

"And that's what makes me mad. The fact that we can accept the deaths of six-year-olds and elders at the rate of one a day makes me furious.

"Those deaths were all from different causes, but they all had this in common: almost none of them would have been dead if there hadn't been a gun, an instant death machine, so easily available.

"Now I understand that there are those who claim that the right to flood our country with guns is guaranteed to them by our constitution. I understand that they think so, although I may never understand why they would want to have so much death around them. I asked you all to meet me here, just outside the Constitution Center, the landmark of our city's most historic accomplishment, to say that the Constitution doesn't give anyone the right to pursue a hobby that keeps the rest of us living in terror.

"I asked you here to tell you that the people who are so upset about broken windshields are behind the times. It's time to get upset about broken, gun-shattered lives.

"I asked you here to tell you that it's time for us to demand that gun owners start to worry about the people instead of the other way around.

"I asked you here, near the spot where the American Revolution against tyranny began, to announce a new Women's American Revolution against terror.

"I asked you here because I wanted to announce one symbol of this Revolution. I want to ask everybody in this country who's fed up with guns and gun deaths and gun-worshipers, to wear a spot of blue on their lapel. I want to ask women to do something extra. When you put on the blue dot, my sisters, let it be a sign that you won't have anything to do with a man who needs a gun to be a man.

"Some of my friends are passing among you now handing out the bright blue button. If you feel like giving them a donation, they'll be glad to pass it along to Handgun Control Inc. or to a special fund for the families of victims of gun violence here in Philadelphia."

A half-dozen attractive youngsters are moving through the crowd, passing buttons to the reporters and the curious. They are mostly the same people we've seen in crowd scenes outside Skipper's, one of them is on roller blades, all of them are in sprayed-on black. We see one woman pulling on a glove, jumping with a dancer's spin, down a step to face the crowd. Paula recognizes her from somewhere, can't quite remember.

"And finally, I want to respond to an article that recently appeared in the Philadelphia Forum. The article said that last February I vandalized a car with a United Gun Association sticker. The accusation is correct. I was the one who Mr. Cardoso saw that night. He saw me at the crude beginning of my determination to make this city safe again."

The crowd of reporters comes out of its stroked-lizard-belly lethargy. Questions are yelled, hands waved. Paula's smile never breaks. She looks like a second grade teacher indulgently timing some planned rambunctious interval. She turns her head slightly to Daniel's side and he pushes forward, between her and the microphones.

"Have a little patience folks, there's even more to come. Paula will take your questions in a minute."

Daniel steps back. Paula is smiling, her smile a little crooked now like she's holding back a laugh. Daniel did it just as they rehearsed it. Her palms are open and angled down, extended to the crowd. She's blessing them, containing them or playing the middle ground between the two.

"There's one more thing. I want to thank Manny Cardoso. You see, I asked him to write that article and turn me in. I asked him to do it so that he could collect the reward and donate it to the brand-new Peace on the Streets Campaign. It was time to move this revolution on to its next stage."

A question squall forms on the horizon, rushes down on Paula. She waits it out, smiling, then resumes.

"I knew that people might be angry with Manny. I knew that it would be hard for him to appear to be a bad guy. I asked him to do it anyway because it was so important and because I knew he had the strength of character to keep silent. He asked me to tell all of you who've been mean to him over the past few weeks that you don't owe him an apology. He says he would have been mean to himself if he hadn't been in on it. He also says that if you'd like to buy him a drink to make up for being mean, that would be fine and that he prefers old Bordeaux."

Paula laughs at her Cardoso joke as if she hadn't rehearsed her speech half a dozen times. For a second she imagines the black and white videotape of Mary Tyler Moore throwing her hat into the cold Minneapolis sky.

"What I want you all to know is that I'm willing to face the consequences of my actions on the night that I broke that windshield. I plead guilty. What I am asking is that all the people who seeded the storm clouds of gunfire face the consequences of their actions too. I ask them to plead guilty in the deaths of the one hundred and eighty-eight Philadelphians who have died from homicidal, accidental or suicidal gunshot wounds in the time since I committed the crime of breaking a windshield.

"All the research tells us that guns are mostly a male problem, so I guess what I'm really looking for is a few real men. Real men take responsibility. Real men don't need stupid little bang-bang toys. I hope the women of America will reject the embraces of the men who need guns to feel like men."

The wind rattles her microphone, snaps her hair across her mouth. Paula pushes it back from her face in handfuls. "I love you all and I wish you safety from the storm."

40.

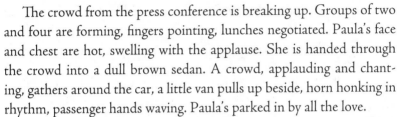

The crowd from the press conference is breaking up. Groups of two and four are forming, fingers pointing, lunches negotiated. Paula's face and chest are hot, swelling with the applause. She is handed through the crowd into a dull brown sedan. A crowd, applauding and chanting, gathers around the car, a little van pulls up beside, horn honking in rhythm, passenger hands waving. Paula's parked in by all the love.

Daniel fusses over a pile of audio equipment, black boxes, gray wires pointing connections. He's not really good with electronics and he has to concentrate. He doesn't know that, trapped in a car between a crowd and a van, Paula is feeling just a little scared.

At the far end of the Plaza, two people are seated on a low brick wall. One figure is wrapped in a black blanket, wearing a giant's black floppy hat and dark glasses. Except for a streak of cleanliness, we would think this creature homeless. Next to him, in black leather jacket and Phillies baseball cap, a figure, black tights, opaque nudity, unmistakably a woman.

"It was hard not telling you, very hard." The voice is Cardoso's.

"Really? How did you keep it in?"

"I promised. I gave her my word. Sometimes when it got really hard, I told myself that someday, when you knew the whole story, you might love me more for it."

Connie is silent, lip-biting. She fights back a tiny sob, swallows air.

Flecks of street trash blowing by them, clouds scuttling and strobing the light. Cardoso drops his glasses. There's a moist residue of the press conference in his eyes, layers of emotion—relief, suspense. His eyes tighten; is he squinting at the brightness or hardening himself against a hit? He decides against waiting, something is going on here, not what he expected, was entitled to, dreamed, for today.

He says, "Look, you stood by me through this while everybody else was treating me like a leper, you were wonderful, you were . . . well, you were the reason I could do it."

Connie braces herself, like she's the one about to be slapped. Her shoulders go up and the bill of her cap drops, obscuring the top half of her face. "I have to tell you the truth. I was playing 'Stand By Your Manny,' but I knew all along that Paula had asked you to drop the dime on her."

"What do you mean? How did you know? Did I talk in my sleep?"

"I tapped your phone."

Cardoso's vision grows gray, he looks inside himself for the rage of invasion, searches for a 'how dare you,' finds nothing. Connie's hands, in fingerless gloves, go to her face. Her wind-stung red fingers poking at tears, blindfolding her, shutting him out.

Cardoso laughs; just belly shakes and breath puffs. "Why the hell are you crying?" he says instead of all the things he might have said.

Connie looks out over the Plaza, we see her in profile, thin elegant renaissance nose like the prow of a ship. "Because this is where you leave me . . . might leave me. I wanted to tell you out here so you could get up and walk away, real clean like. Do you want to know why I did it?"

"Sure. Hey I want to know *how* you did it in case I need to tap your phone someday."

"I was scared." Her words come out in a rush now. "I was falling in love with you." Her eyes dart, birdlike, to us and away. Like a city sparrow she is watching the crumbs and the traffic. Her words slow down, more deliberate now. She breathes with a backward sweep of her shoulders. "Every time I fell in love I got hurt . . . by guys I was good to, guys who shudda loved me and didn't.

"So I asked my cousin's friend to fix me up with this thing and I put it on your phone and that's how I knew all along that you were the good guy in this. I never told anybody and it made me really happy, but I don't want you thinking that I'm sumkinda goddamn saint. Shit, Manny, I can't keep a secret from anybody, how'm I gonna keep one from you."

And so Connie stops talking and from a distance they look like a single black blob with two heads. Connie is knocking her booted heel hard against the bricks. Cardoso reaches out and pulls Connie to him. She falls sideways, chin down, stiff like a tree. She lands in his chest and then there is a tangle of arms and hands on faces and falling hats rolling across paving stones. Manny and Connie are together on their wall.

41.

The next morning, a cab with a crushed left rear fender pulls up and stops in front of Paula's apartment, blocking one of the two lanes on Pine Street. An annoyed motorist blows her horn and then navigates around the cab as Paula gets out. Paula smiles and winks at her, shrugs her shoulders wryly, ain't that lifeinthebigcity.

Then she bows her head to the cab, says, "I'll be right back" to its open window and runs, keys in hand, up the steps to the front door. She's happy taking the steps two at a time, grab a few things, change at Daniel's, off to a newspaper interview. She wonders if there's a message waiting from a certain Ms Garcia-Lane. Am I news enough for you now, honey?

She reaches the third floor, smiling, hours ahead of herself into her day, swinging her keys around her right index finger, breath enough left over to sing some scales if she wanted. There, her door. And before she can bring her keys up to lock level, she can see that she won't be needing them.

The lock's undone, the door is open an inch or so. Paula can see new scratch marks in the old varnish. The locks have been forced, someone's inside. A burglar? No, she knows it's not a burglar. Bastards.

She doesn't know that her lips are pressed together as she pushes the door open with her foot. She has no sense of her fist clenching around the keys into a make-do brass knuckles fist.

"Hey!" she yells as she stamps down into the living room. She'll give them a scare. And of course, there's no one there. She can feel the emptiness, the deadness of the air.

Instead of burglars, there are piles of clothes and books on the floor and the smell of paint. As her eyes adjust to the dim room, she sees that most of the paint is red, big gloppy, poured-from-the-bucket red in action-painter splashes on the floor and walls. It will be a minute before she notices the sprays of blue and white.

Someone has taken her fuzzy pink bathrobe and used it as a swab, dipped it in red and written CUNT in letters two feet high along the wall to her right. The 'T' didn't fit and laps over into the bedroom door.

In the bedroom, she smells chlorine. It's coming from the bathroom. She opens the door and the smell of a hundred swimming pools snaps her head back. The bathtub is filled with water and there's a white one-gallon plastic bottle on the floor marked 'Bleach.' Swimming in her tub are her television, her stereo and a hundred cassette tapes. The hand-written labels on the tapes have already lost their color, no way to tell this chemically erased concert from that newly silent practice. She sees her photo album and a few picture frames in the bottom of the mess and she recognizes the one that held the picture of her and Tom.

The smell is making her dizzy-sick, she opens the drain and backs out of the bathroom, closing the door. She raises the shade and opens the bedroom window.

As she pushes on the sash, she notices another smell. It's—no, it can't be. She turns back to the room. There, in the middle of her mattress is a small pile of human shit.

The little pile seems almost alive in the ruin of her room and it points with its stink to the wall behind her bed. Sprayed in blue is a cartoonish nude of a reclining woman. The hair has been smeared on in red. There is something odd in the drawing of it and Paula comes closer, keeping a nervous eye on the turds on her bare mattress. Yes, there, across the elongated throat, someone has gashed deep marks in the wall and worked in a few more drops of red paint.

And that's when Paula pushes up hard on the window, opens it wide, sticks her head out and screams.

42.

Montage scenes, quick cuts. We hear "This Little Light of Mine," slow and ragged, women's voices, hands clapping the rhythm. Paula's here in groups of women, Paula bright, hair red, blue dot glowing in flocks of grey and brown.

Signs flash by in a rush of hugs and tears.

Ritz Carlton Hotel
Advertising Women Welcome Paula Sherman
Philadelphia Orchestra Central Committee
NWBC

Paula is holding a woman of fifty or so, the woman's face sandblasted red from crying. She is a ruin of grief. They sway together gently, not in time to the music, but to the beat of something else.

A circle of folding chairs, a dozen or so in a high-ceilinged, dirty-white-walled room. Paula, five women in police uniforms, a few more in jeans, one in a suit. Short haircuts all around. They are all leaning, bent over toward the center of the circle. Paula's elbows are on her thighs, her hands bouncing as she speaks, round of heads nodding as she does.

Paula on campus, looking suddenly grown up in the ring of young faces and hands around her.

Paula in the hall of Bethany Baptist; she is standing, down below the altar, singing. Sixty women in a tight pack around her, a few uneasy men at the edges. The women are the source of the soundtrack, Paula's voice is a distinct but subtle thread in their weave. You can hear her if the light shines on things just right. Singing gets tighter, faster, a few voices break off and weave plaits around the melody. Paula is passed, weeping, from one set of arms to another. Paula hugs a skinny girl in an oversized flowered dress. Paula crushed to the chest of a giant. Let it shine, let it shine, let it shine.

New York Review of Literature Vol. XII No. 4

A Modern Lysistrata Takes a Stand in Philadelphia

On the steps of a windy amphitheater in front of this city's somewhat overwrought Constitution Center, a peculiar piece of Aristophanean civic comedy was enacted recently for the benefit of the press.

Attempting to take credit for the wave of anti-gun political action that is sweeping the nation, a young woman named Paula Sherman announced that she, being relatively without sin in a sinfully violent world, had cast the first BB.

Hubristically, Ms. Sherman concluded her diffuse call to action with the hope that American women would don the blue dot and snap shut the doors of Venus for men who recklessly continue to worship Mars.

43.

Back in the UGA conference room, back at the same steel-legged glass table. The floor lighting has been turned off and the ferret man sits in an indifferent fluorescent glow at the head of the table. He is wearing the same tan suit we saw earlier, but his face seems thinner, as though specks of fat and muscle had been extracted from under his cheekbones and around his eyes.

The chubby man is on his right. He seems to have picked up the bits of flesh that his colleague has lost. The ashtray in front of him is empty and the fingers of his right hand are doing a snare drum roll on the table.

The ferret clears his throat. A stalk of shiny hair sticks up from his scalp and waves at the room. "I really don't get it. Everything we've done has been a total screw-up. All of a sudden, this woman's a hero . . . then this "guns aren't sexy" business . . . and if I hear the words "stupid little bang-bang" again . . . Miss Arkwright, what the hell happened with Grass Roots? This story is all over the papers and it's making us look bad. It's expanded, they're talking about all the sponsored citizens' groups that they've turned up and every damn story starts with us. It makes it sound like a little First Amendment support is a goddamn plague and that we started it."

At the other end of the table, Sara Arkwright, composed and lightly tanned, waits with the answer. "We hired Grass Roots to orchestrate phone calls to the top one hundred radio call-in shows. They mostly use actors to make the calls and they pay them pretty well so they figure the money should keep them quiet. Besides, they have firewalls; local dummy agencies and things like that. None of the hired callers would know about Grass Roots itself. I said it must be somebody in their Washington office. I also said we weren't going to pay their bill." A little smile starts at the corners of her mouth and she drowns it with a cough.

The pig-faced man seems to grow redder. He spins the ashtray as the ferret continues. "Lotta goddamn good that does us." He sounds sad, tired. "What about daytime TV?" Sara reaches down below the table. Through the reflections on the glass top, we see her hand holding a stack of letters. "Nobody's interested in us right now. You might want to read some of these replies to our proposal though. Most of them just say that our timing is bad, try again when the dead kid thing isn't news anymore, say six months or so. There is one here from a certain woman with a Chicago TV talk show. It says that the management finds the 'UGA to be strongly anti-child' and suggests they'd have us on when our 'policies are more in line with the needs of families.'

The pig-faced man speaks. He's looking straight ahead, unseeing. "And then there's that goddamn blue dot. That fucking lousy goddamn blue dot." His breaths are shallow, fast and wheezy. His face has a hurt look, a cast of pain that men don't show each other in boardrooms.

"Whatzamatter," the hawk asks, "your wife been wearing one?" His voice is sarcastic and hard.

"No." He draws the word out, shaking his head. "My daughters. My fifteen-year-old brought one home from school. Now the twelve-year-old wants one."

"Jeezis Christ! Pardon my French, Miss Arkwright, but I just don't understand the whole thing." His head is shaking from side to side, the wand of hair trailing behind. "Do you know what those goddamn high-priced detectives found out? They got great video of someone shooting a window right in the neighborhood where it all started. Do you know who's on the video? Mickey Mouse! Fuckin' Mickey Mouse!" His elbows on the table, head in hands. "I don't get it, it's all so . . . so. . ."

Sara leans forward, forearms on the table.

"Goofy?" she says, smiling at him softly.

44.

Night. The sedan, late model and undistinguished, pulls into the space at the fire hydrant on the curb opposite Paula's apartment. The lights go off, the engine stays on.

The passenger, whose door is on the street side, turns and watches up the block for traffic. A minute passes, then two. The door opens but the dome light does not go on. A mostly white car—police—turns onto the street and the door shuts quickly and softly. The passenger's pulse picks up, respiration stops until the car disappears.

The driver reaches for the radio's mike. He speaks, waits, speaks again while the passenger fiddles with gloves and a truncheon, pats the bulk of a pistol into place. A voice squawks on the radio and the driver reaches for the volume knob and nods, once to himself, then again to his passenger, who opens the door and walks heavily across the street and down to Paula's house.

The driver leans sideways and down across the seat. He counts down to Paula's house, then up to her apartment. His eyes go back to his partner who is moving quicker now, at Paula's stoop, almost up the steps. He thinks, as he watches, the same two thoughts that he always thinks. "Pretty springy for a person that size. Ya wouldn't want to be on the wrong end of that stick."

He's feeling some professional version of affection when another pair of headlights turns on to the street: white car, bump on top, POLICE stencilled on the hood. Freeze. As the cop car pulls up, he sees its search light flash briefly on the thick-set body and tight cornrows of his partner, Officer Yolanda Beacon, plainclothes.

The window of the blue-and-white slides down and Officer Beacon recognizes the saggy face of Officer Chickie Schmidt.

"Hey, Chickie!" she says.

"Yo, 'Landa"

"Just checking the front door on 1706."

"Yeah, we saw the incident report, little redhead, right?

"Right."

"She's not home, left with her boyfriend right after we came on. Gettin' a little bang-bang of her own, I guess."

"The cute one with the curly hair? Humph. Awright, see ya."

"Night."

And Officer Beacon climbs the steps, sees that the lock is secure and makes her way back down to the unmarked car, nodding to her partner as she goes.

Paula misses all this action. She and the cat are staying at Daniel's now. But she can't miss the constriction in her throat, the pressure in her chest, the little tangy taste of fear. When Cardoso's article came out, she quit her job at Odetta. She is now nothing but the shots that she used to fire, her present has no particulars.

A few people love her, a few more hate her, nobody knows her. Sort of like before, but more intense. She likes the intensity and it wears her out. She often smiles at Daniel and thinks to herself, "Oh, Tom."

45.

A crowd of men, mostly young, some walking west, some east in the sunshine on Walnut Street across from Rittenhouse Square. They are headsetted to radios and they seem to be moving to the same rhythm.

There's a man sitting on an indigo milk crate on the corner. He is middle-aged and pale, wrapped in an overcoat to ward off spring. He is cradling an old battery-powered radio and there is a cardboard sign in front of him that says: Street Musician with no Talent please Help

Listen. The street sounds disappear and we hear music, sweeping, undulating, insistent. It's the beat to which every man on the street is marching. The music fades and a voice from the radio says,

"Hello, this is Dr. Judith Sills on 1440 AM. Are you ready to do good? Are you ready to do better?" The woman's voice is liquid velvet decorated with bugle beads. She-class. It sounds like sex in high places, like wisdom all dressed up for a party.

And the score of men say, " Hiya dahkka judy, yeah umphup all right I am."

"And we have a caller."

"Hi, Dr. Sills, this is Rochelle." Robert sits slowly, knowing that he missed his big moment.

"Hello, Rochelle, and welcome to 1440."

"You always ask people to call in with great moments and I have one."

"Yes, Rochelle, thanks for calling 1440. What's up?"

"There was that woman. Paula, you know, the one with the BBs . . . well, maybe I should say that I was mugged three years ago. The mugger fired a gun near my ear. I've been a little deaf and a lot afraid ever since. I don't really go out alone at night, and there's always this tightness in my stomach."

The voice, that voice, says, "Tell me when you feel that tightness." But the men on the street are gradually, in ones and pairs and bunches, talking to themselves, a Babel-babble of fears and triumphs and sick knotted gut muscles.

More voices, more fears, the sounds of them, peak to trough, even each other out. It would be white noise, but it's black noise, yellow noise, jews' noise, goys' noise too.

And the voice from the radio says, "Yes, yes I know how horrible that can be and I'm going to tell you what to do. The fear never goes away, but you can take control of it and taking control begins when you, aah, when you start to fight back against the things that make you scared. Now Rochelle, I'm going to give you some suggestions, some things to bring out the brave in you."

The Braves, of course, are in spring training now and the American anthem is just winding down.

"Oe'r the la-and of the free

And the home of the brave."

The starting pitcher is nineteen, chisel-faced, whip-bodied, we zoom in on him as the stadium quiets and as he checks the sign. There's a blue dot embroidered over his right breast. He winds up and the crowd sounds are women sounds, squeals and roars. His motion to the plate is high and over the top. Fast ball inside corner.

"Strike one!"

46.

Four voices and a lute.

First there was darkness all around
Then there was a lightening
Then Old Adam mired in sin
And finally a brightening.

"And now, it's time for the greatest force in the history of the media, Imus in the Morning."

The screen brightens and we see a car radio partly blocked by a white Styrofoam cup. The image on the screen is vibrating slightly. The car, we are to conclude, is in motion.

"Our guest today is Daniel Farber who really isn't who we wanted to have at all. Last week I was watching Tom Brokaw fumble his way through the news, a disgraceful spectacle if there ever was one, anyway I heard him say, 'Tonight's feature: How guns lost their cool.' Then he went on to talk about this woman in Philadelphia who lost a friend in a street shooting and decided to take on the United Gun Association by shooting out the windows of its members' cars.

"I found this mildly amusing because if ever there was a bunch of cretins who deserved to have something blown out . . . well, we tried to get this woman on the show, this, um, Paula Sherman, but she turned us down flat and stuck us with, um, one Daniel Farber. So, Daniel, what do you have to with all this?"

"Well, Don, it says on the blurb that I'm Paula's legal adviser, I guess that's PR talk for designated boyfriend. You were lucky enough to get me because Paula has decided that she only wants to talk to women about this."

"So, Daniel, were you out there popping windshields with Ms. Sherman?"

"No, I-man, I wasn't. In fact the minute Paula told me what she had done, I advised her to lay down the gun and come clean. By the way, I should point out that although there are a lot of rumors, Paula has admitted to attacking only one UGA decal."

"Were you going out with her at the time she was doing her little vigilante stunt?"

"Yes, I was."

"And you had no idea?"

"None. None at all."

"That's kind of hard to believe, Daniel. As an attorney, wouldn't you be obliged to turn in anybody who was committing a crime?"

"That's true, I-man, but I had no idea what she was doing. When we started dating, the last thing I was interested in was her marksmanship."

Knowing chuckles.

"So you and Paula have become, ummm, minor pop culture icons. Will we be seeing you on those papers in the supermarket checkout line?"

"Actually, we were hoping we could both become famous, you know, mom and pop culture icons."

Manly groans.

"But that's another story," Daniel continues.

"And one I hope you'll refrain from telling."

"Anyway, Paula was approached by the *American Enquirer* and we may do something with them, and there's been all this ridiculous stuff with agents and Movies of the Week. One guy even tried to tell us that if Paula would sign with him, he'd see about getting Michelle Pfieffer to play her, but Paula's holding out for Rosie O'Donnell. She says that way people won't be so disappointed when they meet her in person."

"I notice that you and Ms Sherman aren't campaigning for any particular gun legislation."

"That's right. We think that's a waste of time right now. The gun interests have most state legislators bought and paid for. We're hoping to change a cultural climate. We're telling America that only cops and dorks own handguns, so if you've got a gun and you're not a cop, you're a dork."

"And what about this blue dot business? If you walk down Fifth Avenue at lunchtime, it seems like every woman's wearing one."

"It's not just Fifth Avenue, it's Main Street. The blue dot is certainly the hottest thing on college campuses too. I don't know where this is going, but if a lot of men have to make the choice between sex and guns, well, we might find out what this gun fetish is all about."

"There's another thing. Your Miss Sherman doesn't refer to 'guns' any more, she calls them 'bang-bangs.' The phrase seems to have caught on. What's that about?"

"Well, I guess it's her way of reminding everybody what stupid little toys guns are."

"Now, Daniel." Imus's voice is warmer now. "I don't remember people getting so worked up about guns when I was a kid."

"I-man, things are different now, flintlock rifles weren't exactly weapons of mass destruction. "

Guffaw.

Gunslinger

Jimmy got a bang-bang
bang-bang bang-bang
Ka REEM got a bang-bang too
How much can ya figger
Yo' jigga wid a trigger?
What the fuck ya gonna do?

Well, Keefa come to witness
that ya got us scared shitless
You keep the people down
with your gun and your frown
and you actin' like a clown
in yo' little part of town

Ya think ya got a gold mine
tek-nine, all mine
Think that yo bad and yo nothing but sad
And you looking kinda silly
with yo four-inch willy

Well, Keefa come to witness
that ya got us scared shitless
You keep the people down
with your gun and your frown
and you actin' like a clown
in yo' little part of town

Now lookee uppa here, right around this mike
See all the gold stuff, the hot stuff the wet stuff?
Ain't that the stuff you like?
It's the stuff'll make you cry
Stuff good enuf to die
It's the creamy, it's the shaky
It's the chocolate and the bakey

So guess what little brotha?
You stupit little motha
with a gun for a brotha
No matter what you do,
(slowly, points to her breasts)
Ain't none of this for you

(whispers)
Jimmy got a bang-bang
bang-bang bang-bang
Ka REEM got a bang-bang too
How much can ya figger
Yo' jigga wid a trigger?
What the fuck ya gonna do?

47.

Daniel's voice calling. "Hey honey! C'mere! Quick!"

In Daniel's apartment, Paula's TV set is on the counter between Daniel's kitchen and dining room. The set looks clean, simonized, up in the world. Paula and Daniel are together, with cable.

Paula's feet slap the hardwood floor as she enters from the left, towel-drying her hair. She's wearing a floppy white t-shirt with the word HOBART across the chest: one of Daniel's kitchen machine series. The shirt clings damply to her here and there.

"Whuz." her voice is muffled by the hairbrush handle between her teeth.

"Shhh . . . it's Clint Eastwood . . . an interview."

Paula wiggles her way into a spot on the couch beside him.

On the TV screen layers of warm colors float from side to side. An off-camera voice asks the actor about the .357 magnum that he carried in the movie Dirty Harry, recently sold to a collector at auction.

Eastwood's eyebrows go up, his face filling the tiny screen, he squints as if he's seeing something on a ridge far off in the distance.

"It was a prop gun of course. We don't keep handguns around the house. This one was sort of a joke, enormous, ominous, as a prop, it was a caricature of a character who was only half-serious himself." He pauses thoughtfully, looks to the side.

"The man has timing," Daniel says.

"That's not all he's got," Paula wiggles again, this time moving closer to Daniel.

"I always saw the guns in my films as metaphors for thoughtlessness, ironic metaphors. When I heard that Christies was doing a movie memorabilia auction and they had some other weapons, well, it seemed like a good time to get rid of it. I donated the money to Handgun Control."

"The gun from *Dirty Harry* sold for eighty-eight thousand dollars. That's a very substantial amount of money. Isn't it odd that someone whose movies were often violent would support a cause like Handgun Control to the tune of eighty-eight grand?"

"You know, not all my movies were gunslingers. I think the best film I ever made was *Bird* . . . the good guys and the bad guys were all on the inside . . . that man's weapon was a saxophone and his only victims were his wife and himself."

Switch to a long shot. Clint is wearing a tweed jacket over a black shirt open at the neck. There's a button on his lapel: a small light circle with a dark dot in the center. Is it blue? The picture is in black and white but Paula and Daniel are screaming and hugging, can-it-be eyes wide with rectangular TV highlights, bouncing on the couch. Daniel lunges for the set, hoping he can turn a knob and will the colors back to true. The phone rings and he grabs it.

Breathless seconds. "Yes we are . . . his lapel . . . ? no, the dot . . . yes it is itisitis, yes it's blue." And Paula and Daniel are dancing in each other's arms, her shirt riding up and more and more of her bare skin pressing against him with every step.

48.

The images of women and children at play slip down and across the screen, pages from a happy scrapbook. We are looking at a film on an Ultra High Definition Television screen, the colors shimmering, deliberately weird, inviting Junkfood-Chrome. The name OPRAH appears, changes typeface, slips, slides and rotates, grows, shrinks, changes font again.

Dissolve to a cheering, clapping, whistling studio audience in a TV amphitheater. The shape of the room bounces all the sound to the center of a small stage. At that focus is a medium-sized brown woman, smiling. She's wearing a yellow silk suit that wraps her body with the grace of very expensive clothes. Her face is beautiful in an open, easy way. She is holding a microphone as if it were a present. Just for you.

Over the applause, she turns to the camera and invites us in to her private consideration.

"Would you break the law?"

Head turns to half profile, mouth corner turns down, reciprocal eyebrow arches. Applause fades and Oprah asks the question again. We don't respond, so she turns to the studio audience again.

"Would you break the law?" Emphasis shifting to the "you."

"Would you?" A ragged volley of no, a yes or two, a murmur, was that a maybe?

"Almost a year ago in Philadelphia, a woman went on a rampage, shooting out car windows with a BB gun . . ."

Oprah's voice fuzzes out to a soft buzz. We see in quick collage Tom and Paula on the street, the shot, the auld lang syne execution, the senator's ad, uncle Sammy Claus, UGA decals dissolving in spiderweb cracks, Anvil Chorus eight bars, Michelle's funeral.

Back to Oprah's audience, a snapping sound, Paula is wearing a suit in British Racing Green, skirt cut high. She is standing a little to the right of center stage, strong-legged, smiling as if she just got the joke.

Perhaps a fifth of the women rise at once with military quickness. To the tune of "For the Lord God omnipotent reigneth" from Handel's *Messiah*, they sing:

> It's wrong to DES-troy someone's pro-PER-ty,
> Yes IT'S wrong
> Yes IT'S wrong
> It's very very wro-ong.

And then they sit. Lady in the front row, breakably young, turtleneck, stands up stiffly. Chants My KID'S seven years OLD seven years OLD. Her head pushes forward, lips popping out the emphasis. Other voices off-camera:

> Mine TOO.
> Mine TOO.
> Mine TOO.
> Mine TOO.

Black woman, solid in a blue pin-striped business suit, snaps to her feet, staccato chants:

> Those guns
> What do they NEED them for?
> What do they NEED them for?

The neat line of her buttons is jerked and gapped by her arm swings. Camera shifts to large blonde woman, lots of hair, big glasses. She is nodding her head and applauding with big seal-flap gestures.

Oprah's eyes are right on the camera. "I want to ask you, America, yeah you, honey, will you join with us, with Paula and me, to get rid of those stupid little bang-bangs and make the streets safe for our children? Paula, do you have any more of those buttons?"

And Paula, seeming surprised by such a good idea, looks upstage and down and finds a two-pint woven basket. She finds a button, looks doubtful, Oprah points to her bosom on the side away from the camera. Paula blinks and swallows and fumbles a pin through a couple thousand dollar's worth of silk.

Oprah flares her nostrils, turns to us. We see the pin. It's the blue dot and the camera pans in, veering from Oprah and closing in on Paula whose face fills the screen.

49.

The security guard in the back of the Oprah building is folding his silver-sided sandwich wrapper into ever smaller triangles when Paula comes down the stairs from the green room. She is red-faced, damp, alert, hyper-on, ready for anything.

The guard looks at his screen, clears his throat.

"Ms. Sherman?"

"Yes."

He looks at her, then down at his screen. Yep, it's her, redheaded white chick.

"Your car's outside, you're going back to your hotel? The Lakeside?"

"Yes, I have a radio interview tonight and I thought I'd get some rest and call home and . . ." She realizes that he's not listening. The interview is over.

The heavy wire mesh door that separates her and the guard from the outside world buzzes at her and swings open.

"Down the steps and to your left."

"Thank you." She starts to say something else, stops herself and walks through the door which closes metallically behind her. Down and to the left is a door, another guard and a blast of afternoon sunlight. The car, black and shiny like a ripe olive, has its door open for her and another guard is standing, smiling, palm up, directing her in.

But there's a crowd at some barricades on the sidewalk to her left and another across the street and Paula stops to smile and wave at the twenty women and babies who wave back and blow kisses. She sees a hand-lettered sign that says Guns Do Kill People

Underneath the lettering there's a photograph of a boy in a graduation cap and gown. Another woman is wearing a t-shirt with the words bang-bang free zone in a single sans-serif line across her breasts. She spots a woman holding up a baby in a pink sleeper. Woman and baby are both wearing blue dots and she moves toward them. The guard's arm turns over, palm down. He points.

Across the street the crowd is older, male, organized. They stand in two rows, signs in front. When Paula sees them, she hears the bullhorn.

". . . second amendment . . . leave our homes unprotected."

One man at the flank is giving her the finger. She turns back to the guard, ducks into the car and collapses, sprawling, knees spread across the back seat. She looks toward the crowd of men, reads the last words of one sign:

. . . my cold dead hand

She turns away, back toward the guard. He winks at her and gives a thumbs-up. She notices that his eyes flick down and that he's looking at her legs as the car pulls away and makes a right turn. Paula closes her eyes and has a vision of a hotel room, hot shower, Daniel, room service.

Paula looks back, as if she could decode the strange scene with an extra glance. A car, pale green and compact, has made the turn behind her and the driver is honking the horn and someone is waving from the front passenger seat. But Paula is suddenly weary and turns forward, looking over the driver's blue-suited shoulder at the street.

At the first stop light, she sees a couple, young and chatting, looking bored and comfortable. The woman is short and solid, pale and dull. The man is lean and delicate, a head taller than the woman. She is wearing a pea coat, he has a leather jacket. Paula is about to tell herself that the man looks a lot like Tom when she realizes that she's lost the memory image she had of him. It's bleached like the photo floating in her bathtub. She can see the shadows, but she has to invent the highlights.

Shit. She turns back to the rear window, to the carload of friends behind her. Maybe they could all go to Skipper's for a drink. Her treat. And then she notices the other cars, two of them, black and wallowing on soft springs. One of them blows its horn as it races through a stop light. The other pushes forward next to the green car. Can he be trying to run them off the road?

"Driver?"

"I see them. That sometimes happens when you leave Oprah's, autograph hunters, groupies."

"I don't think these guys want an autograph."

The driver's hands tighten on the wheel, she can see him checking the rearview mirror. He slows, makes a sudden right turn then accelerates. Two blocks, hard left. Paula is thrown on the first turn, braces herself for the second. Looking out the back window, she can see one of the black cars, then the green then the other black.

The driver slows for the entrance to Lakeshore Drive, checks the traffic and floors it through the red light. The first black car checks his chances, speeds up then slams on the brakes as the Drive traffic cuts him off.

"That should give us a minute or two, it's a long light."

Paula looks back, sees the little green dot and the line of traffic as her friends. "You're going to the Lakeside, right?"

"Right."

It's just up ahead, after that pink building.

"Stop!"

"We're almost there, I . . ."

"No, stop. Stop here, in that driveway." Her voice is high-pitched, panicked, and the car pulls off the road, behind a line of poplars, half hidden. Paula opens the door and lurches toward the road. At the curb, she turns back, closes the door. The driver is out now, looking at her, seeing the wild look in her eyes. He's scared for her and he comes around the car toward her. Paula lowers her head and runs, off the curb and onto the blacktop of Lakeshore Drive.

The three cars have turned now and the driver of the first black car sees Paula leap in front of a white sedan a hundred yards ahead. He thinks he hears the brakes, as its driver panic-stops. Later, he will tell certain people that he saw Paula flying.

He'll be wrong of course, she was jumping into and then across the center lane of traffic onto the median. As he pulls onto the shoulder, he sees her hop down and cross the opposing two lanes in a second. Her skirt, he remembers, is hiked up and she looks barefoot.

The green car stops ahead of him, then the other black a little further on. There's a line of people alongside the road now, jiggling, hopping, watching traffic, timing their chances.

Paula's off the road and on the grass, running toward the lake. She wishes she could apologize to the driver in that white car. She slows to look over her shoulder and she watches the line on the curb collapse into a double vee as they make their way across the road, running after her.

She feels her feet slipping on the grass as she turns away, jogging toward the lake. She can hear a siren as she reaches the rocky beach and as she slows down, its rhythm takes her. Breathing just a little harder than usual she looks out over the water. The siren and the sounds of running feet compose themselves into a hum behind her. She takes a few more steps and, standing ankle-deep in the freezing water, Paula raises her arms and starts to sing.

About the author

Lynn Hoffman

Lynn Hoffman's writing might be described as adventuresome, sensitive, sexy, eclectic. Eclectic might also describe his many credentials: Ph.D. in anthropology, award-winning writer, executive chef, and expert in fine wines.

Lynn Hoffman is widely published, which makes us very pleased he chose Kunati Books to publish his latest breakthrough novel.

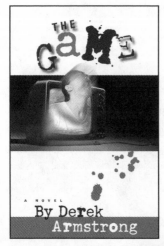

KÜNATI

Provocative. Bold. Controversial.

The Game
A thriller by Derek Armstrong

Reality television becomes too real when a killer stalks the cast on America's number one live-broadcast reality show.
■ "A series to watch ... Armstrong injects the trope with new vigor." *Booklist*
US$ 24.95 | Pages 352, cloth hardcover
ISBN 978-1-60164-001-7 | EAN: 9781601640017
LCCN 2006930183

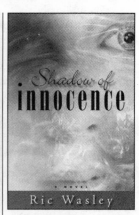

Rabid
A novel by T K Kenyon

A sexy, savvy, darkly funny tale of ambition, scandal, forbidden love and murder. Nothing is sacred. The graduate student, her professor, his wife, her priest: four brilliantly realized characters spin out of control in a world where science and religion are in constant conflict.
■ "Kenyon is definitely a keeper." STARRED REVIEW, *Booklist*
US$ 26.95
Pages 480, cloth hardcover
ISBN 978-1-60164-002-4
EAN 9781601640024
LCCN 2006930189

Whale Song
A novel by Cheryl Kaye Tardif

Whale Song is a haunting tale of change and choice. Cheryl Kaye Tardif's beloved novel—a "wonderful novel that will make a wonderful movie" according to *Writer's Digest*—asks the difficult question, which is the higher morality, love or law?
■ "Crowd-pleasing ... a big hit." *Booklist*
US$ 12.95
Pages 208, UNA trade paper
ISBN 978-1-60164-007-9
EAN 9781601640079
LCCN 2006930188

Shadow of Innocence
A mystery by Ric Wasley

The Thin Man meets *Pulp Fiction* in a unique mystery set amid the drugs-and-music scene of the sixties that touches on all our societal taboos. *Shadow of Innocence* has it all: adventure, sleuthing, drugs, sex, music and a perverse shadowy secret that threatens to tear apart a posh New England town.
US$ 24.95
Pages 304, cloth hardcover
ISBN 978-1-60164-006-2
EAN 9781601640062
LCCN 2006930187

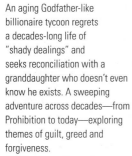